CLUB TIMES

For Members' Eyes Only

An offer Joe Turner can't refuse!

After a heavy gossip session in the Yellow Rose Café, I've made it my mission to nail down Joe Turner to the fine town of Mission Creek. Sure, you can describe his bedroom eyes and broad shoulders until your tongue goes dry, but this won't be worth beans if he goes back to the Midwest. We know who to contact if we need cement blocks, but that's only for drastic measures, Mr. Del Brio.

Meanwhile, I'm feeling in the mood for some sunshine. The closest I get is when calling Tyler Murdoch so I can listen to his tales about the hot jungles of Mezcaya. He keeps hanging up on me, thinking that I'm breathing too heavily into the phone, but we know how cold it can get in Texas, and darned if I'm not the only one who has respiratory ailments this time of year.

Nadine Delarue's bronchitis nearly killed us all.

Let's welcome Marisa Rodriguez to the fold. We're happy to have you as a new member of the Lone Star Country Club! And congratulations on snagging one of the hunkiest bachelors in Mission Creek!

Get ready to *spring* into action at the Lone Star Country Club. We are happy to serve you...Texas-style!

About the Author

JUDY CHRISTENBERRY

was born and raised in Texas. While she'd participated in some continuity stories, she'd never had one set in Texas. When she heard about the LONE STAR COUNTRY CLUB program, she asked to be included. The continuity stories draw from all kinds of experiences. She was once a foreign language teacher (French) and it helped out this time creating a character who was new to America.

"Writing entertains the writer as much as the reader," she says. As the mother of two daughters, she finds everything in life contributes to the store of information that she uses in her stories. "Even difficulties teach us new experiences. Thanks for the opportunities."

JUDY CHRISTENBERRY

THE LAST BACHELOR

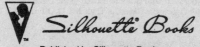

Silhouette Books

Published by Silhouette Books

America's Publisher of Contemporary Romance

Special thanks and acknowledgment are given
to Judy Christenberry for her contribution
to the LONE STAR COUNTRY CLUB series.

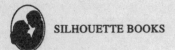

SILHOUETTE BOOKS

ISBN 0-373-61360-1

THE LAST BACHELOR

Visit Silhouette at www.eHarlequin.com

Printed in U.S.A.

Welcome to the

LONE STAR
L*C
COUNTRY
CLUB
EST. 1923

*Where Texas society reigns supreme—
and appearances are everything.*

**The last remaining bachelor of the five Turner men
has come home...and has found himself falling
for his new green-card wife.**

Joe Turner: In order to protect an Estonian damsel-in-distress—and get his well-meaning family off his back—Joe shocked the Turner clan by marrying Ginger Walton aka Virvela Waltek. The marriage-in-name-only worked out so well that everyone fell in love with his new bride...including Joe!

Ginger Walton: Being surrounded by Joe's family was better than anything Ginger had ever imagined. But it was nothing compared to being wrapped up in his arms! After fleeing a terrifying situation, Ginger felt safe with Joe. But how much longer would Ginger be able to pretend her feelings for her soon-to-be "husband" were only make-believe?

Mission Creek Crisis: Luke Callaghan has returned to Mission Creek and received nothing short of a spectacular hero's welcome. However, his joy is short-lived when he learns about the kidnapping of little Lena...his daughter!

THE FAMILIES

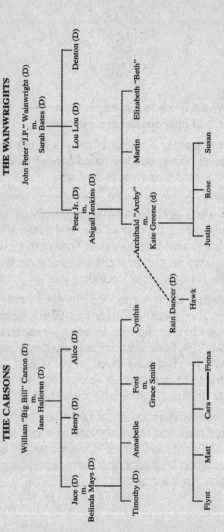

THE CARSONS

William "Big Bill" Carson (D)
m.
Jane Halloran (D)

- Jace (D)
  m.
  Belinda Mays (D)
- Henry (D)
- Alice (D)

- Timothy (D)
- Annabelle
- Ford
  m.
  Grace Smith
- Cynthia

- Flynt
- Matt
- Cara ━━━ Fiona

THE WAINWRIGHTS

John Peter "J.P." Wainwright (D)
m.
Sarah Bates (D)

- Peter Jr. (D)
  m.
  Abigail Jenkins (D)
- Lou Lou (D)
- Denton (D)

- Archibald "Archy"
  m.
  Kate Greene (d)
- Martin
- Elizabeth "Beth"

- Justin
- Rose
- Susan

Rain Dancer (D)
- Hawk

D   Deceased
d   Divorced
m.   Married
- - - Affair
━━━ Twins

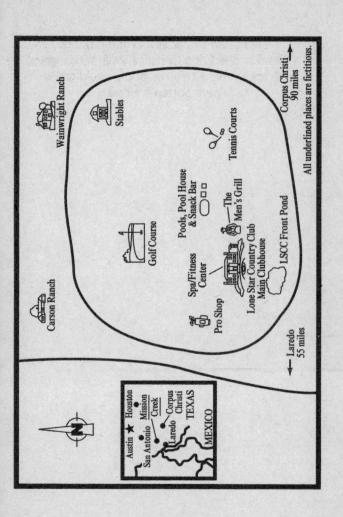

Wainwright Ranch

Carson Ranch

Stables

Tennis Courts

Pools, Pool House
& Snack Bar

The Men's Grill

Golf Course

Spa/Fitness
Center

Pro Shop

Lone Star Country Club
Main Clubhouse

LSCC Front Pond

← Laredo
55 miles

Corpus Christi
90 miles ↑

All underlined places are fictitious.

N

Austin ★   Houston
San Antonio   Mission Creek
   Corpus Christi
Laredo

TEXAS

MEXICO

Dedicated to Barbara White-Rayczek,
a friend in deed, and Christina Willi, my daughter.
Without those two, my book would never
have gotten finished.

Prologue

She froze, her hands full of orders ready to deliver to the latest table of diners.

Her heart pounded in her suddenly tight chest. She couldn't breathe. Nor could she think. What should she do?

Dashing back into the kitchen, she set down the plates of food and grabbed another waitress. "I have to leave. I feel very sick. Can you take these orders to table number seven? They're big tippers," she added as an incentive.

"I've got a lot of tables myself," the waitress complained.

She dug her hand into her apron pocket and pulled out five dollars from her tip money. "Here, keep this, too. I'd really appreciate it."

Then she dashed out the door that led to the parking lot, assuming the food would be delivered. Right now, she had more to worry about than the people dining at the Lone Star Country Club.

She'd known this day would come. She'd prepared for it. But, oh, she'd prayed—hoped—that there would be a miracle in this blessed land of the free.

But no. Today it had ended.

One

Joe Turner drove up the drive of the Lone Star Country Club. It was a little late for lunch, which meant the café wouldn't be packed. Maybe he'd have a little time to chat with his favorite waitress.

He chuckled. He was a fool, of course. Ginger Walton probably wasn't even twenty-one, and he was thirty-four. If he were precocious, he could claim to be old enough to be her father. Nevertheless, she caught his eye.

And every other man's in the place.

It wasn't her curves that drew all the men's attention, though Ginger certainly had some striking ones. It wasn't even her auburn hair, beautiful complexion or her big blue eyes. It was all of those things, actually, but it was her appearance of innocence that touched every man's heart. At least it did Joe's. He always had the belief that she was a princess in disguise who needed rescuing.

"Right," he muttered, telling himself he was crazy.

The well-groomed drive wound its way to the entrance of the country club. Joe was almost there when out of the corner of his eye he caught the color of the waitresses' yellow aprons they wore in the Yellow Rose Café. One of the waitresses was running from the parking lot toward the main highway.

Almost immediately he realized it was Ginger, her smooth hair blowing away from her face as she hurried. He knew she didn't have a car, but usually she caught a ride with one of the other girls. Besides, he knew she worked until nine o'clock on Fridays.

Joe picked up speed and followed the circle up the other side, toward the highway. He pulled in front of Ginger and stopped, hurrying out of his car to intercept her.

"Ginger? Is something wrong?"

"Oh, Mr. Turner! No. Nothing is wrong."

"Then why are you crying?"

She self-consciously wiped her cheeks. "Uh, I—I don't feel well. I must go home." She started around him.

"Get in my car. I'll drive you home."

"No, I—" As she looked back toward the country club, she evidently changed her mind. "Okay."

Joe looked behind Ginger and saw two men in dark suits getting into a dark car—a government car from the looks of it. With a frown, he slid behind the wheel again as she got in.

"Who are they?" he asked. He turned to look at Ginger, only to discover she'd slid down in the seat, as if she were hiding. "Ginger, what's going on?"

"I—I can't— Please just take me home."

Her normally pale cheeks were flushed and tears gathered in her light blue eyes. Joe could never refuse to help her. He put his Lexus in Drive and started toward the small apartment where Ginger lived. When he'd first realized Ginger lived in such a tiny place, he'd tried to talk Harvey Small, the manager of the club, into giving Ginger a pay increase so she could afford a nicer apartment.

Joe didn't like Harvey, but the man assured him Ginger was making good money. It wasn't his fault she didn't spend her pay on better accommodations.

Joe drove slowly, studying Ginger out of the corner of his eye, trying to figure out what was wrong. She didn't give him any clues.

"Are you nauseated?" he asked.

"No." She stared straight ahead, her teeth sunk into her bottom lip, a frown on her face.

"I could take you to the doctor."

"No! I—I just need to go home."

"Okay," he agreed, trying to sound calm. But something was wrong.

They approached the small apartment house, and Joe figured he'd done his best for her. She obviously didn't want any help.

Suddenly she moaned. "No! No, no, no!"

He stopped at once. "Ginger, what's wrong? I'll help if you'll tell me."

"No one can help me now." Her mournful words broke his heart.

"Sweetheart, I promise I'll do what I can."

"Take me to…the park, please." She had her eyes closed. Then she opened them and hurriedly said, "If you don't mind."

"Not at all." The small park across the street from

the apartments had a few picnic tables and a basket-ball court that drew the neighborhood boys after school. Right now it appeared deserted.

He parked his Lexus in the empty parking lot. When he turned around, he saw Ginger staring into his rearview mirror. That was when he noticed the dark sedan parked near Ginger's apartment. The same car from the country club.

"I think it's about time you explained to me what's going on. Obviously those two men are up-setting you. Shall I go talk to them?"

"No!" she shouted, then seemed to pull herself together. "Mr. Turner, you've always been so nice, so generous, I know you want to help. But there's nothing you can do. If you don't know what's wrong, then you can't be accused of anything."

"Accused? Accused of what? There's nothing il-legal about giving a ride to a friend."

Ginger looked at the man beside her with grati-tude. An architect from Chicago, Joe had come back to his hometown a few months ago to supervise the rebuilding on the country club, after a bomb had de-stroyed the Men's Grill restaurant. He'd been friendly ever since the first time she'd served him. Ginger had loved waiting on him not only because he was handsome, with mahogany hair and chocolate eyes, but because he treated her with respect. He didn't try to get familiar with her or ask her out. Now he called her his friend.

But she couldn't get him in trouble. With a sigh, she suggested he go back to the country club.

"Are you coming with me?"

"No, I can't."

"So what are you going to do?"

She didn't have an answer for him. As long as those men were there, waiting for her, she couldn't go home. And she couldn't leave until she got her money out of the apartment. Why hadn't she put it in a bank? Instead she'd cashed her paychecks and hidden in her apartment the money she didn't need to pay bills. All so she could leave quickly when she had to.

"Ginger?"

It took her a moment to remember Joe had asked her a question. What *was* she going to do? "Uh, I don't know."

"Are those men looking for you?"

"They are looking for Virvela Waltek," she admitted with a sob.

Joe frowned at her. "Who's that?"

She sniffed. It was so very hard to admit the truth. Finally she whispered, "Me."

She didn't want to look at him, expecting him to be horrified by her deception. When she looked at his handsome face, however, she didn't see disgust.

He leaned closer. "I knew you had a little accent, but I couldn't identify it. Where are you from?"

"Estonia. I came to America three years ago. I was sixteen." It seemed so very long ago.

"Good Lord, you're only nineteen?"

"Almost twenty."

He smiled ruefully. "I'm fifteen years older than you."

She shrugged her shoulders, as if that didn't matter. It wasn't as if he was romantically interested in her. A good-looking man in his prime, educated, wealthy, Joe Turner could have any woman he wanted.

"So, are you here illegally? Is that why you're scared?"

"Not really. But…my mother has refused to sponsor me now."

This time she had shocked him, she could tell.

"Your mother? Your mother sicced the INS on you?"

Ginger nodded, keeping her gaze lowered. It was such a shameful thing, for her own mother to turn her back on her. She'd warned Ginger, of course, thinking it would make her come home and do what her mother wanted her to do. But it hadn't.

His stomach growled and he apologized. "I'm sorry, I'm hungry. How about we go to the Dairy Queen and grab something to eat?"

"No. They would find out that you hid me."

"Sweetheart," he drawled, and she almost grinned. She loved it when he sounded like John Wayne. "They won't think I know your identity. Besides, they won't think to look there."

"I can get out now and you can go back to the club and have a nice meal." She was determined to do the right thing for this kind man.

He started his car and backed out.

"Wait, I have to get out."

"Nope. You don't even have a sweater to keep the chill off."

Usually late March in this part of Texas was warm, but a storm had come through the day before and the wind was still blowing, the air chilly.

"Please, I can—"

"Come with me." It was more an order than a request.

Two minutes later he pulled into the Dairy Queen and led her inside. "Let's take the back booth. No one will see us there."

She obediently slid into the booth, facing the door.

"I'll be right back," he assured her. He ordered some food at the counter and came back to join her.

"Now, tell me why your mother would try to get you thrown out of the country. That seems pretty weird to me."

"It is better that you know nothing. I shouldn't have told you my real name. When they ask you questions, you must say you think I am Ginger."

"Maybe they just have some questions for you and that's all. I don't see why they'd want to kick you out. You're a model citizen."

Her chest constricted. "I—I don't have a sponsor. My mother wants me to— I won't."

"Won't what?"

"Please, Mr. Turner—"

"I think you should call me Joe, don't you? You're not waiting on my table now. We're talking.

We're friends. Friends call each other by their first names."

Before she could protest, one of the employees brought over a tray of food and put it down on the table. "Here you go," the woman said. "Need anything else?"

"No, thank you," Joe replied. After the woman walked away, he grinned at Ginger. "She doesn't quite have your style, but the food's hot. I got each of us a hamburger. You haven't eaten, have you?"

She shook her head.

"There's French fries, too, and a Coke." He gently shoved her food toward her. "You have to eat so I don't feel bad eating in front of you."

She took the food. Who knew when she'd have a meal again? She'd best be practical.

Joe was relieved that she accepted the food. She was looking pretty fragile. After she'd had several bites, he asked casually, "What is it your mother wants you to do? And where is she?"

Ginger looked up from her food. "She's in New York. She married a man there."

"So she got her citizenship because she's married to an American? How long has she been married to him?"

"Three years. He came to Estonia and he proposed. We came to America three months later and they married at once."

"She knew him before?"

Ginger shook her head.

Joe stared at her. She was a beautiful, delicate

young woman. If her mother looked anything like her, he wasn't surprised that a man would marry her at once. "So why would she want to send you back to Estonia? She might never see you again."

Tears pooled in her blue eyes again and she looked away.

"You've got to tell me, sweetheart. Otherwise, I can't help you."

"You can't help me, anyway. My mother will not change her mind."

"Just tell me," he urged softly, reaching across the narrow table to lay his warm hand over hers.

"She wants me to marry."

"Whom?"

Her cheeks flushed again, as if the information shamed her.

"Do you know him?"

She nodded her head, but she didn't look up.

"You don't love him?"

"No!" When he didn't speak again, she finally said, "My mother married a man who is a member of the mob in New York. I believe that's what you call it, right?"

"Yeah," he said grimly. He didn't like the way the story was going.

"My stepfather's friend is his boss. He decided I would make a good bride, but I said no."

"How old is he?"

With her head still down, she whispered, "Fifty-eight."

"Damn!" Joe cursed. That kind of a marriage was

barbaric, trying to force a beautiful young woman into a marriage with a man three times her age. "You were right to refuse."

"Even if it means my mother is beaten?" When she lifted her gaze to him, he read the guilt and pain there. He squeezed her hand.

"It's not your fault."

She looked away. "I was eighteen. I believed all the wonderful things they say about America. I thought I was free, that I could choose." She sobbed, before she could compose herself. "I ran away."

"Good for you."

His reaction seemed to surprise her, but the thought of her being married to an old man, one involved in crime, made his gut clench. "I think if we explain the problem to the government men, they won't send you back."

"They will," she assured him, fear in her eyes. "I must go away where they can't find me."

"Ginger, I don't think you can hide that easily. You'll need to work. They'll be able to find you."

"I saved all I could. I can make it for a while."

"Let me contact a lawyer. There's got to be a better way."

"Lawyers are very expensive. I cannot—"

"One of my brothers is a lawyer. He'll help us." He took a bite of his hamburger, but he kept his gaze on her.

She shook her head. "I don't want other people to

be punished. I don't even know your brother. I cannot shift my troubles to him. Or to you."

"Ginger, I want to help."

"No. I must go." Without waiting for his agreement, she slipped out of the booth and headed for the door, leaving her food uneaten for the most part.

Joe stared after her. Then he wrapped up his hamburger and fries, grabbed his drink and hurried after her. By the time he got to the car, she was nowhere in sight. But he couldn't stop trying to help her. Getting in his car, he drove the two blocks back to her apartment. He scanned the area and didn't see the government car. Maybe they had given up and returned to wherever their office was located.

He found a parking place. Leaving his food in the car, he locked the door and headed for Ginger's apartment. He only knew which it was because he'd discovered Ginger walking home one Friday night and had insisted on driving her home. He'd even walked her to her door, telling her it wasn't safe to just drop her off.

He knocked on the door. "Ginger? It's Joe. Let me in, please."

She opened the door slightly. "Go away, Joe. I'm packing."

"Don't go, Ginger. I can help you."

"No, I can't—"

"Miss Waltek?"

The two men in dark suits were standing behind Joe, staring at Ginger.

Joe saw panic on Ginger's face and regretted his attempt at intervention. Maybe she would have gotten away if he hadn't held her up. But he knew better than that. Besides, a life on the run would be hard for her.

Her head fell, and she stared at her feet. Then she looked up. "Yes, I am Virvela Waltek." She stuck out her wrists, as if she expected to be cuffed.

The men stared at her in surprise. "We just wanted to ask a few questions. May we come in?"

Her expression blank, she moved back and nodded.

After the two men had stepped around Joe and entered the apartment, they tried to close the door.

"I'm coming in, too."

"Who are you?" one of the men asked.

"Who are you?" Joe demanded in return. After all, the men hadn't identified themselves.

"I'm Carl Fisher and my partner is Craig Caldwell. We're INS officers. And you?"

"Joe Turner, a friend of Ginger's."

"That is not her name," Fisher pointed out.

"It's what I call her." He wanted to plow his fist into the man's face, but reminded himself they were only doing their jobs. Still, if they tried to shut him out, he would fight them.

"Miss Waltek, do you mind if he comes in?" Fisher asked.

"He hasn't done anything wrong!" she exclaimed.

"They know that, sweetheart. I just want to be with you, in case you need me. Okay?"

She nodded.

Joe shut the door behind him, looking around at the flimsy table and four chairs, one beat-up sofa and an old lamp. When Ginger said nothing else, still looking panic-stricken, he gestured to the table and chairs. "Shall we sit down?"

The two agents turned to the table and Joe reached out for Ginger's hand. "Come on, honey." He led her to the table and took the seat beside her, keeping her hand in his.

Fisher folded his hands on the table and leaned forward. "Miss Waltek, your mother has informed us she is withdrawing her sponsorship of you for citizenship. Can you tell us why?"

Ginger said nothing, only shrugged her shoulders.

The other man, Caldwell, added, "Your mother has told us you are working as a prostitute."

"No!" Ginger slammed the table and stood up.

"Gentlemen," Joe began, keeping his temper with deep breaths, "that is not true. I've known Ginger for the past six months. I can vouch for her."

Both men ignored him and stared at Ginger, who reluctantly sat down.

"Why would your mother say such a thing?" Fisher asked.

"She—she is trying to force me to come home," Ginger said, her voice trembling.

"Tell them everything, honey," Joe urged. "Tell them the truth."

"Yes, tell us the truth," Caldwell encouraged.

Ginger stared at the table, visibly swallowing, before she spoke. Then, shaking, she explained why her mother was trying to force her to return to New York.

"The mob? You mean the Mafia?" Fisher asked.

Joe stepped in. "Yeah. Look, the man her mother wants her to marry is fifty-eight! And her mother is being beaten because Ginger ran away."

"Beaten? A woman can get a divorce and keep her citizenship if she's being abused."

"He'll kill her," Ginger whispered.

Joe's feelings toward Ginger deepened. This poor kid didn't have many choices. She was so alone.

"Can't something be worked out?" he asked.

"Maybe," Fisher replied. "But we'll have to take her with us."

Ginger pressed her back against the dilapidated chair, as if trying to get far away from the agents.

"No!" Joe shouted.

Caldwell bristled. "Now, sir—"

Joe stared at Ginger, trying to prepare her for what he was going to say. "She can't leave. We're planning to be married. But Ginger wanted to wait until she was a citizen."

"I'm sorry, sir, but—"

"I'll take her to Vegas tonight and we'll get married. Then she can become a U.S. citizen, right?"

"Unless we determine she married only for that reason." Fisher stared at him. "And you'll have to remain married for a year."

"I already told you we're planning to marry. Give us twenty-four hours and we'll answer any of your questions. Ginger will be my wife and nothing can be done to her, without an investigation. We'll pass any test you give us, right, Ginger?"

She stared at him, her mouth open.

TWO

"Did you plan on marrying this man?" Fisher asked Ginger.

Joe held his breath. Would she understand what he was offering? Could she play the role of an adoring fiancée?

"Yes. But I felt ashamed to come to him without my citizenship. I thought it would be better to wait," she said, her cheeks inflamed. "I didn't want him to be ashamed of me."

Apparently her response had the right tone because the two agents looked at each other and then stood. Fisher said, "Excuse me a minute. My partner and I have to talk."

Knowing the men were watching them even as they moved to the door to confer, Joe leaned over to Ginger and brushed his lips over hers. "Don't worry," he whispered.

Ginger stared at him, questions in her gaze, but he couldn't say anything now.

The two men came back to them. Fisher, obviously the senior partner, said, "Here's the deal. We'll give you a week. If you appear at our office with a legitimate marriage certificate, we will give you a temporary green card, Ms. Waltek. Then, sometime in the next three months, you'll be called in for an interview. If you pass the interview, you'll receive your permanent green card.''

"Perfect," Joe agreed, a big smile on his face. He noticed that Ginger simply stared at them.

Fisher looked directly at Joe. "But if she disappears," he warned, his tone serious, "we will file charges against you, Mr. Turner, for helping her escape." He turned to Ginger. "Do you understand, Ms. Waltek? Your friend will go to jail if you run away."

In a whisper, she said, "Yes, I understand."

Five minutes later, Ginger and Joe were alone.

"We lied!" Ginger whispered, as if she thought the two men might be standing on the other side of her door, waiting for them to emerge.

"But it was for a good cause," Joe assured her. "Why don't you find something to change into, and I'll call Harvey and get you a couple of days off. Or I can give him your notice if you want."

"My notice?" she asked.

"You know, let him know that you're going to quit your job."

Her eyes grew even larger and panic filled her face. "No! No, I must have a job. Please don't!"

"But, Ginger, we'll be married. You won't need to work." He squeezed her hand again, and realized he liked touching her. "I know you've been taking night classes. Now you can go to school full-time."

"No! I must continue to work. I must pay for myself. I can't shift my difficulties onto you. I won't run away, so you won't get in trouble, but I may have to go back to Estonia soon if we don't— I have another week. I must work all I can.''

Joe gave her a strange look. What was wrong? She had promised not to disappear.

''You have to take a couple of days off so we can go to Vegas.''

''Vegas?''

''I mean Las Vegas, the place where people go to get married quickly. We can leave tomorrow morning and be married before evening. Then we'll come back the next day. After that, you'll have at least three months. You can earn more money.''

''I can't allow you to make such a sacrifice. It will shame you, and your family.''

''No, it won't. Actually, it will help me.''

She frowned. ''How can that be?''

''Because I'm the only guy not married in my family. Everyone's been setting me up with blind dates and insisting I bring a woman to family occasions. They're driving me crazy. Now I can take you, and everyone will be happy.''

Ginger stared at him. Why was he not married? He was a handsome man, educated, not like that beast her mother wanted her to marry. How could Joe have no lady in his life? She stared at him.

''Don't worry, Ginger. I know I'm too old for you. I'll let you go after the year when your citizenship is official. It's just so you get your green card.''

''You would do that?''

"Of course."

She dropped her head again, trying to think. The panic still lingered, making it difficult to think clearly. "I must call Daisy."

"Why?" Joe asked.

"She—she's my friend. We tell each other things."

"Does she know about your being from Estonia?" he asked, sounding like he might be jealous if Daisy knew her story.

"No. I didn't tell her everything. I didn't want her to get in trouble."

"Then don't tell her until we return."

"But—"

"I'd like to invite her to come with us as your maid-of-honor, but Harvey would kill me if I took his two most popular waitresses away at the same time. Now, you start packing. Pick something comfortable to wear on the plane, jeans or something, and pack your fanciest dress for the wedding ceremony. I'll call Harvey."

"Are you sure?"

"Absolutely."

Joe stood there, watching Ginger as she crossed the room and opened one of two doors. It was a small closet, but there wasn't a lot in there. She pulled out a small cloth bag, then a simple blue dress and some sandals.

She hesitated, looking at him, and he hurriedly picked up the phone. He didn't want to make her self-conscious by staring at her.

He was amazed, however, at how right saving Ginger seemed. He'd always picked up strays as a boy, bringing them home to feed and care for. His mother had believed he'd grow up to be a doctor, but he'd turned to architecture to satisfy his artistic side. He'd once considered becoming a starving artist, though his fiancée had protested his choice and had eventually left him for a man with more money. Joe had concentrated on his career as an architect to show her she'd made a mistake.

He'd avoided women for a while, but then he became the ultimate bachelor. He enjoyed the companionship of many women, but he planned no future with any of them. Ginger, he reminded himself, was too young for any real interest. He was rescuing her, that was all.

"Let me speak to Harvey Small," he said to the club receptionist when she answered the phone. When Harvey picked up, Joe launched into the reason for his call. "Harvey, this is Joe Turner. I need to borrow Ginger for a couple of days. Is that a problem?"

Harvey didn't take the request calmly. He poured out demands and questions that Joe had no intention of answering. "I'll explain later," he said.

That response didn't satisfy Harvey.

"Two days, Harvey. That's all I'm asking." Joe pulled out the heavy artillery. "Would you prefer her to quit?"

"No! But I don't see—"

"Harvey, slavery was abolished a long time ago.

Ginger has some rights. Now, she'll be back at work on Monday, and that should be enough to satisfy you.''

With that, he hung up the phone. He didn't even worry that Harvey might fire Ginger. Joe didn't want her to work, anyway. However temporary their marriage, she would be his wife. And he would take very good care of her. For a little while, at least, Ginger would not be alone.

Ginger stared out the window of the plane, her brow furrowed. ''Are we still in the United States?''

''Of course, honey. Why would you think we weren't?''

''When we flew to America, it was a long flight. Is America really this big?''

''It's a lot bigger. Didn't you fly to Texas when you ran away?''

''No. I—hitchhiked,'' she said carefully.

''Lord have mercy, that's dangerous. You didn't get hurt, did you?''

''No, the people were very nice.''

''Don't ever do that again. There are some evil people out there.''

''No, Joe, they were very kind.''

''I'm glad, honey, but you're my responsibility now. I don't ever want you doing that again.''

''But we are not really—''

Joe covered her mouth with his hand to stop her from finishing her sentence. He leaned closer and whispered, "We don't ever tell anyone, even strangers, that our marriage isn't, uh, normal. Okay?"

Her eyes big over his hand, she nodded.

He released her and sat back, drawing a deep breath.

After a moment, Ginger leaned closer to Joe. She whispered, "Won't everyone think it strange that we came to this place to marry? They will wonder why, won't they?"

He took her hand in his, realizing he had a lot of questions to answer. Clearly, Ginger had concentrated on her work and her classes at the junior college, but knew very little about American culture. "You'll see when we get there. A lot of people go to Vegas to marry. No one will think anything about it."

He believed that, as long as she didn't say the wrong thing. But he'd be on his guard. Maybe if she said something inappropriate, he'd stop her by kissing her. That would make everyone believe they were newlyweds.

His heart rate tripled just thinking about kissing Ginger. She was so beautiful, so naive and unprotected. He loved the idea of protecting her. He'd never seen himself in the hero role, but it was enticing, especially when he saw that emotion in her gaze. He lifted her hand to his mouth and kissed her smooth skin.

When she jumped in surprise, he leaned closer. "People will expect me to touch you, Ginger. Try not to act so surprised. In private I'll leave you alone."

She frowned. "You will?"

"Yes, of course. I promise."

"But I will be your wife."

His heart beat faster. "Yes, but not—" He stopped himself. Great. Now he was the one having problems with their secret. "We'll talk later."

The pilot spoke over the loudspeaker. "We're now approaching Las Vegas airport, so please be seated and fasten your seat belts. Thank you for flying with us today."

Joe leaned over and snapped her seat belt.

"I can do it," she protested gently.

"I know, but I like to help you. In a few minutes we'll be on the ground. Are you excited?"

She met his gaze briefly, then looked away. "Of course." She thought that was the answer he wanted. But she hated the idea that she was trapping him into marriage.

Joe was a kind man, offering her his protection. She must try not to take advantage of him. Some of the men at the club, especially when they were in the Men's Grill temporary facilities, where their wives never appeared, were eager to take advantage of her, not to protect her. But she'd always turned them down. She'd never had to turn Joe down. He had never seemed interested in her in that way.

She sent up a small prayer that she would never shame Joe, that she would repay his kindness with loyalty and patience.

The pilot set the plane down smoothly, and when they were parked at the gate, Joe stood in the aisle to gather their luggage from the overhead bin.

Her cloth bag looked shabby beside his sleek leather one, but he showed no concern about what people might think. "Come on, Ginger. Time for us to go."

She slipped out of her seat and stood beside Joe, ready to go where he led her.

Much to Ginger's surprise, they didn't take a taxi when they exited the airport. A man was standing on the sidewalk with a sign with Joe's name on it.

"Does he know you?" she whispered to Joe as he waved to the man.

"No, honey, I hired him to meet us."

"Oh."

The man opened the back door to his limo and waved for her to enter. She slipped onto the seat and stared, then scooted over as Joe followed. "Joe, there's room for many more people," she whispered as the car began to move.

"Yeah, but it will just be the two of us. So we can have privacy."

"But everyone is staring."

"Don't worry, they can't see us. Now, we're going to go to fill out papers and then find a marriage chapel. They'll have a room where you can change. Is that all right? You have your dress ready?"

"Yes." Her dress was a simple sheath in pale blue

that her mother had made her for her own marriage to Harold, Ginger's stepfather.

Something in her voice must have worried Joe. "Should we go shopping first and buy you a new wedding gown?"

"No! It would cost a lot of money. It's not necessary."

He gave her a strange look. "I have plenty of money, Ginger. You don't have to worry about that."

"The bride is supposed to pay for the wedding."

"No, you have that wrong. The bride's family is supposed to pay. And since you don't have a family, I'll take care of everything."

She said nothing else, but she determined to keep down the cost of their wedding. After all, he was doing her a favor.

By the end of the evening, Joe was frustrated. All he'd bought her was a small bouquet of flowers. But he had to admit Ginger looked beautiful in her simple dress. The pale blue color complemented her auburn hair and blue eyes. And the ceremony, although brief, achieved their goal.

Afterward Ginger was ready to get back on a plane and return to Texas.

"No, honey, I made us a reservation. We have the honeymoon suite at the Bellagio."

"What is that?"

"It's one of the hotels on the strip."

When she discovered the suite consisted of a huge space with a tub big enough to hold half a dozen people and several bedrooms and a living area, she told him they should ask for a smaller place so they could save money.

He refused. He needed plenty of room so he could handle the desire to put his arms around her. Especially as the sun went down.

"Will we leave in the morning?" she asked anxiously.

"Our flight's around noon."

She frowned and said nothing.

"We're going to dinner in ten minutes. Okay?"

"Why don't we eat here? Look at all this fruit." She gestured to the delicious-looking fruit basket on the cocktail table. "That would be enough for dinner."

"Not for me. Besides, a wedding dinner is traditional."

She kept frowning.

After dinner, Joe took her to the casino. He changed dollar bills into coins and handed her some, explaining she should put one in a slot machine. She slipped the coin in. He told her to pull the handle.

She did so and waited.

With a kiss on her smooth cheek, he said, "Sorry, you didn't win. Here's another one."

She stared at the coin he held out and then at him. "Why?"

"To try again. To see if you win."

"But I didn't."

"So you try again."

"No! I will not give your money away."

"But it's supposed to be fun." He waved his arm. "All these people are playing the slot machines. Don't you want to?"

"No. A good wife does not give her husband's money away," she assured him, a determined look on her face.

He sighed. "Okay, we'll try again later. Do you want to see a show?"

"What kind of show?"

He tried to explain what was available. The only thing she showed interest in were the famous white Bengal tigers, but that show was sold out.

Finally, he had an idea. "How about art? The Bellagio has an art gallery with famous paintings. Would you like to see them?"

Her eyes glowed. "Oh, I would love that. One day in New York I got to go to a museum. The paintings were beautiful."

Joe shook his head in amazement and took his bride to the art gallery. Slowly they looked at the paintings. In college, Joe had studied art, along with architecture and in his spare time did some sketching. But he enjoyed the evening more than he had thought he would, mostly because Ginger liked looking at the paintings, too.

But he didn't think anyone else would believe him. A night in Vegas with no gambling, no alcohol and no sex. He'd ordered a bottle of champagne for their wedding supper, but Ginger had preferred Coca-Cola. No bright lights, big stars or crowds of people. Just art, whispered comments and privacy.

After the gallery, Ginger was ready to turn in. "Do you mind?" she asked. "I'm tired. So much has happened in two days."

He put his arm around her shoulder and led her to the elevator. "You're right, honey. Will you be okay if I come back down for a while?"

"You like to gamble?" she asked, surprised.

"Sometimes." Like when I have to leave you alone, he said to himself. Otherwise you couldn't keep me from your side.

With a cautious smile, she told him good-night once they were in the suite. He kissed her cheek and turned away. "I'll be back in a little while."

She nodded and disappeared into the big bedroom.

Wearily, he turned away. He didn't want to gamble. But he'd go put in an hour on the slot machines, or maybe blackjack, to pass the time. Then maybe he could go to sleep without thinking about Ginger in the massive bed in the next room. Or, maybe more accurately, about *joining* her in the big bed.

He hadn't realized resisting temptation would be so difficult.

When Joe awoke the next morning, about nine, he showered and shaved, then dressed before discovering Ginger poring over a book in the living room.

"What are you reading?" he asked.

Ginger looked up in surprise. "Oh! I didn't know you were awake. I'm studying history. I have a test Tuesday night."

He shook his head. That wasn't something he'd

brag about: his wife studying while on her honeymoon. "Ready for some breakfast?"

She agreed, though she said she'd eaten some fruit when she got up at seven.

"I thought you'd sleep late."

"No, I usually get up at seven. Do you sleep late every morning?" she asked.

He shook his head. "I guess I just stayed up too late last night." Actually, he'd stayed downstairs until the early morning, trying to tire himself out.

"Did you lose a lot of money?" she asked, that frown already in place.

"No, in fact I won."

The frown disappeared, but she didn't show any greedy elation.

"So come on," he urged her. "Let's get some breakfast. I can pay for it with my winnings."

"I can pay for myself. I didn't pay my share for dinner last night."

Joe huffed. "I'm the husband. I'll pay for our meals."

"But that's not fair. You're helping me. You shouldn't have to pay."

He studied her clear eyes, her earnest expression. Crossing to her side, he took her shoulders in his hands. "Ginger, if we're going to convince people that we are truly married, we're going to have to act like it. I'll pay for our living expenses. You'll take care of cooking occasionally, cleaning a little. That's how it works."

"But—"

"No arguments." With a sigh, he said firmly, "Honey, I'm an architect. I make a lot more money than you. I can afford to take care of you." He turned her around to face the door. "Now, I want no more arguments about who's going to pay. Let's go get breakfast."

By the time they'd had breakfast, packed up and got on the plane, Joe had a lot better picture of what he faced when he got his bride back to Mission Creek.

Heaven help him.

Three

Joe called his mother when they changed planes in San Antonio. They were only a short flight from Mission Creek.

"Mom, it's Joe. Are you and Dad going to be home this evening?"

"Why, yes, dear. Where are you?"

"I'm in the San Antonio airport. I have someone I want you to meet. May we drop by in about an hour?"

"Of course. Will you have eaten?"

"No."

"I'll have some food ready. Is this a friend from Chicago?"

"No, it's better than that, Mom. I'll see you in an hour."

He hung up the phone and found Ginger staring at him. "What is it? Why are you upset?"

"Why did you tell your mother?"

"Well, actually, I didn't. We're going to surprise her," he said with a big grin. His family would definitely be surprised. And he would be relieved. He'd told his family he'd never met a woman he wanted to marry. The truth of the matter was, he didn't think he'd ever want to risk his heart again. He'd been betrayed when he first fell in love, and it had become a habit to avoid commitment. But marrying Ginger wasn't real. And she truly needed him.

"But I don't think we should tell your mother," Ginger said.

Joe sighed. "Remember we agreed to talk and act like we're really married. We wouldn't keep it secret. It'll make my mother very happy, I assure you."

"But she will be upset when we don't stay married."

Joe looked around to be sure no one important had overheard Ginger's words. "Look, Ginger, you mustn't say things like that."

She covered her lips and looked around, too. "Joe, I don't think we should've done this. I'm afraid you will get in trouble."

Joe shook his head. "Too late. Come on, our plane is leaving."

"But I'm very hungry," she complained. "I can pay for—"

He swooped down and kissed her. Then, pretending touching her lips had been normal, he said, "No need. Mom is fixing a meal for us."

Ginger wore a shocked expression on her face. He didn't think the kiss would elicit that much of a surprise. But in the future he was going to have to be careful, because kissing her, he'd discovered, was a real pleasure. He leaned closer, drawing in her scent. "Remember, we're married."

He didn't give her a chance to respond. He took

her hand and led her to the gate where the small plane awaited.

Ginger sat quietly for the next forty-five minutes, greatly relieving Joe's mind. Once they settled into a routine, things would be easier. But they weren't there yet.

He'd left his car at the small airport. It took only a few minutes to reach it since their luggage was carry-on. Right on time, he pulled up to his parents' house. All the cars parked in front told him his brothers and their families were there, too.

He had to warn Ginger, though he knew she wouldn't like it. "Uh, Ginger, I think my entire family is here tonight. Remember we have to act like we're married."

"You have a big family?"

"I have four brothers. I told you they're all married. Only one doesn't have any children yet, but his wife is expecting in two months. Just be careful what you say."

She nodded, though she tightened her lips and set her shoulders, as if she were about to face a hostile crowd.

"And try to look happy," he added, thinking she might burst into tears at any moment.

They got out of the car and he came to her side. "Are you okay?"

"Yes, of course."

When they reached the front door, he hugged her close. "Everything's going to be great, honey." He aimed a kiss for her cheek, but she turned to look at him and his lips landed on hers. The contact surprised both of them. On impulse he pressed his mouth against hers, encouraging her to open to him, as if they were lovers. Even more surprising, Ginger didn't pull away. He pulled her closer, wanting more, and her arms wound around his neck.

He heard the front door open and his mother gasped several times. But he didn't care. He was kissing his wife.

"Joe! Who is this?" his mother asked.

He released Ginger, his gaze still on her face. "This is my wife."

Ginger found herself the center of attention, as questions flew fast and furious around her. Joe's mother seemed happy, his father stared at her and the rest of the people, his brothers and their wives, wanted details.

"Where did you two meet?" one Turner wife asked.

Ginger replied, "At the country club."

"Oh, are you a member, too? I haven't seen you."

"No, I'm not a member. I work there as a waitress." Though she figured that would upset everyone, she couldn't lie.

Another woman, who looked vaguely familiar, stepped forward. "Oh, you're the waitress who's so patient with the children."

"You're right," another woman said, then turned to Ginger. "I remember you now. I'm Amy, Bill's wife," the woman said, holding out her hand.

As Ginger shook her hand, a man stepped up alongside Amy. "Hi, I'm Bill. I'm Joe's oldest brother."

Ginger nodded. She stared as the other brothers sorted themselves out and introduced themselves and their wives.

"What's your last name?" someone asked.

She opened her mouth to say Walton when Joe intervened. "Turner, of course."

Joe's father, who introduced himself as Ed, stepped forward. "Welcome to the family, Ginger. You're mighty pretty."

"Th-thank you."

His mother, Vivian, herded everyone to the dining room. "Come along now. I fixed a late dinner for these two and snacks for everyone."

"Good. Ginger was starving in San Antonio. I know she'll be glad to eat," Joe said, beaming.

Actually, Ginger's hunger had disappeared once she became the center of attention. But to be polite, she nodded and took Joe's hand and followed everyone else. As she looked at Joe, she wondered why he'd kissed her on the front porch. Had it been for show, or did it mean something to him? And would he repeat it?

Once all the adults were seated around the table, with the children playing in the living room within sight, the questions began again.

"See any good shows in Vegas?" one of the brothers asked.

Ginger looked at Joe, hoping he'd field the questions. She was getting so nervous, she didn't think she could eat and talk at the same time.

"Nope. We were only there one night."

"Too much to do, huh?" his brother responded, using his elbow to share the joke with his brother beside him.

Ginger didn't exactly understand what was so funny. Except that she was starving and too afraid to eat.

"Did you gamble?" one of the other brothers asked. Ginger looked at Joe, hoping he'd provide the answer again.

"Nope. Ginger was too concerned about losing her husband's money," Joe told them with a grin. Then he added, "Hey, guys, give Ginger a chance to eat. She can't talk and eat at the same time."

"Joe's right," Vivian said. Then she turned to Ginger. "And I think you did the right thing, not gambling away Joe's savings."

The other men roared with laughter. "Yeah, poor Joe, he's always broke," one of them added.

Ginger was horrified. She stared at Joe. Why had he insisted on paying for everything?

"Let's change the subject," Joe suggested. "What happened while we were gone? Any word on that stolen baby?"

Joe was sitting next to Ginger and he felt the tension rise in her even more. He hadn't thought anything would be more terrifying than his family. He looked at Ginger sharply as his father answered his question.

"No, no word on the baby. I'm beginning to think the mother stole her. Maybe changed her mind about giving her up."

"No!" Ginger exclaimed. "No, she wouldn't do that!"

Everyone stared at her. Joe tried to think of something to say, but fortunately his sister-in-law Amy came to the rescue.

"I think Ginger's right. That's not something a mother would do. I agree, Ginger."

"Me, too," his mother agreed. "But I'm sure someone will find the baby soon, unless…"

Joe was afraid Ginger was going to cry, though he didn't know why. "Uh, did I tell you they're scheduling the reopening of the Men's Grill at the club for next Saturday? I'm proud of the work I did, along with Jenny. I hope you're all going to be there."

Ginger looked at him. "Who is Jenny?"

Joe's eyebrows shot up. Ginger almost sounded like she was jealous. Maybe she had more acting ability than he'd thought. "Jenny Taylor. She's the interior designer who's been working on the Men's Grill with me."

"Oh."

Bill, Joe's longest-married brother, said, "Don't worry, Ginger. She's nice, but you're prettier. Besides, Joe chose you."

Ginger tried to smile, but she wasn't very successful.

Joe slid his arm around her. "You bet I did. I've had my eye on Ginger ever since I got back."

"You sure didn't let any of us in on it," his father pointed out.

"I wasn't going to introduce her to my brothers until after I had a ring on her finger."

"Oh, I forgot to look at your ring," Kitty, his youngest sister-in-law, exclaimed.

Suddenly all the gazes in the room were fixed on Ginger's left hand. Ginger proudly wore the plain gold band Joe had bought her in Vegas, but Joe knew what to expect.

"What happened, Joe?" Bill exclaimed. "Did all your investments crash?"

Ed coughed, and Bill turned to look at him. "You're embarrassing the newest Mrs. Turner, son."

Ginger looked at his mother, and Joe leaned over to whisper, "They're talking about you, sweetheart." Then he couldn't help himself. He kissed her again, lightly this time, since everyone was looking.

"I'm planning on buying her some diamonds, but we did this so suddenly, I didn't want to buy diamonds in Vegas. I'll go to the jewelry store here in Mission Creek tomorrow."

"You need any help, ask me, son," Ed offered.

When his brothers all protested, Joe grinned and held up one hand to quiet them. Then he turned to his father. "No, Dad, I've got it taken care of." Joe looked at Ginger, who sat silently.

As his brothers continued to tease him, Ginger said softly, "I don't need diamonds. Joe is—"

Afraid she was going to say the wrong thing, he

kissed her again. "Thanks, sweetheart. See, guys, I didn't marry a greedy woman."

His mother congratulated him.

"Are you sure you don't want to spend the night here?" Vivian Turner asked one more time.

Joe had already refused her offer once, which was a great relief to Ginger. She wanted to go home and get ready for work tomorrow. She was exhausted.

"Thanks, Mom, but I think we'll get settled in. And thanks for dinner," Joe said.

Ginger hurriedly thanked her also. Not that she'd eaten much. Her nerves were strung so tight, she couldn't. But she had peanut butter and crackers at home, which would hold her over until tomorrow.

Once inside the car, she lay her head back on the headrest, trying to calm down. All in all, she thought, the day hadn't gone too bad. Joe's parents and his brothers were nice people, good people, who had tried hard to make her comfortable. And she had been—until Ed mentioned the kidnapped baby.

Ginger hoped her reaction didn't red-flag anyone's attention. But she knew the baby's mother hadn't stolen her back. She knew because the baby's mother was her best friend and fellow waitress at the Lone Star Country Club, Daisy Parker.

She stole a glance at Joe, checking his facial expression, as if he could read her mind. His eyes were steadfastly on the road ahead.

Ginger recalled the day Daisy had confided in her that she was baby Lena's mother and had had no choice but to leave the child on the golf course where she knew she'd be found, and then taken care of. Ginger hadn't judged her friend, only offered comfort to the obviously distraught woman.

She told no one about Daisy—with one exception—and she silently admonished herself for revealing the truth to a man who'd held her at knifepoint in the lot of the country club a couple of months ago. But she'd been terrified and afraid for her life. Now, again, Daisy's secret was safe with her, she'd tell no one, not even Joe.

As if to steel herself in her vow, she took a deep breath and let it out in a sigh.

"You okay?" Joe asked. "It's been a long day. I bet you're exhausted. I'm sorry about all the commotion tonight. I'd thought it would just be Mom and Dad."

"It was very nice," she said, staring through the windshield.

"How about we go straight home tonight? Tomorrow we'll take care of things."

"Yes, thank you."

She wasn't sure what those things were, but she was ready to call it a night—until she realized Joe had missed the turn to her apartment.

"Where are we going? You needed to turn back there."

"No, sweetheart. My condo is two more blocks ahead. I live in the Blue Shades complex."

"But I do not!"

Joe sighed. "We're married. That means we live together."

"But I don't have clean clothes. And I need my uniform for the morning," she said firmly, feeling like an idiot for not realizing what was going to happen.

Joe turned at the next street corner and headed back the other way. "Okay, we'll go to your place and you can pack what you need for tomorrow. We'll get the rest of your stuff later."

"Do you have enough room for me?"

He grinned at her. "I have a lot more room than you do. By the way, where do you sleep? I never saw a bed."

"On the sofa. It's called a futon."

He shook his head.

"What?"

"You'll have your own bedroom at my condo. I have three bedrooms, so it will be just fine. I promise."

When they finally arrived at Joe's condo, he unlocked the door and swung her up into his arms. She clutched him around the neck. "What are you doing?"

"It's a tradition in America. The groom carries the bride over the threshold of their first house." He carried her into the place and set her down, giving her a kiss that wouldn't be easily forgotten. He was breathing a little heavily when he stepped back.

"But we're aren't—"

"Shh. I don't need to kiss you again this soon.

But I'll have to if you're going to say anything inappropriate.'' He grinned, trying to convince her he was kidding. But she took a couple of steps back.

"So what do you think?'' he asked, waving his arm to indicate he was asking about his condo. It was well designed, with blue-and-cream-colored decor. Ginger began to prowl around. When she came to a door, she would ask permission to open it. His bedroom didn't receive much inspection, but the other two bedrooms, with a bathroom between, were closely examined. The kitchen, however, received the most attention. It was large, with modern appliances, all sparkling clean.

"This is beautiful!'' Ginger exclaimed.

"I'm glad you like it. I've designed my dream home, but since my move to Mission Creek was temporary, I didn't see any point in building it yet. This condo has been fine for me.''

She gave him a strange look. Then she asked, "Which room shall I use?''

"Either one. But I think the second one is larger. Tomorrow we'll pack up your apartment and see if we can get your deposit back. Did you pay first and last month?''

She nodded.

"Okay, I'll talk to the manager. I'm going out to get your bags,'' he said, and turned toward the door.

"I can go get them.''

"No, honey, that's another thing husbands do.'' And he disappeared.

She sat down in the living room, unable to believe

she would be living in such a beautiful home. The slate-blue carpet was thick, two couches faced each other with a large square coffee table in between. Lamps and decorative items filled the room. Her mother's apartment in New York City was dingy and small, nothing like this.

"Did you decide which room you want?" Joe asked as he came in with her bags.

"The second room is fine." She hurried over to open the door. "The bed in here is so pretty." It was queen-size, with a beautiful comforter and pillows on it. She couldn't wait to get in it.

"Thanks. Jenny picked out the coverlet. She said it reminded her of a flower garden."

"Yes, it does," she said a little stiffly. "Joe, will she understand about me? I do not want to cause you trouble."

He turned around to stare at her. "Jenny? Why wouldn't she?"

She shrugged her shoulders and sighed.

"I should've taken the leftovers Mom offered. You're exhausted and you ate hardly anything." He turned and left her in the room by herself.

She started to follow him, but she decided she'd apologized enough. Instead she decided to unpack. Her clothes barely made a dent in the deep bureau and roomy closet. She gathered clean underwear and her nightgown and deposited them in the connecting bath.

She came back out and went into the living room again. "Is it okay if I take a bath?" She was so looking forward to it. Because the tub in her apartment was narrow and rusty, she had only taken showers since she'd come to Texas.

"Sure. I ordered pizza, by the way. It'll fill you up so you can get a good night's sleep. For breakfast tomorrow, I have cereal. But afterward we'll go grocery shopping and get what you like."

"I can eat cereal."

Joe eyed her speculatively. "Ginger, earlier tonight did you think my brothers were teasing me because I didn't have money?"

She hesitated. "Maybe."

"Honey, they were teasing me because I don't usually *spend* a lot of money. I have that reputation, but it's only because there's just me. I have money, I promise. Certainly enough to buy groceries."

"I can give you my rent money."

"Now, don't start that again. I told you how marriages work. I pay the bills, okay?"

She nodded, remembering the wifely duties he'd pointed out. She'd have to be sure she did everything as he wanted. To be able to live in such luxury for even a few months would be worth hard work.

"Go get your bath and then come out. The pizza will be here by then."

He'd ordered pizza because he thought she might be hungry? That seemed the height of decadence. She loved pizza, but she only allowed herself to order it once a month, on her day off. Usually, she worked seven days a week. Harvey didn't mind, and she'd been saving her money. When she worked, she got two meals at the club, and she usually skipped the other one.

She went into the bathroom and began running the water, delighted when no rust came out as it did in her apartment. Then she heard Joe's voice. She hurriedly turned off the taps, afraid she was using too much water.

"I only used a little. I'm sorry," she said as she opened the door.

"What? Use as much as you want, honey. It's okay. I wanted to tell you there's a bottle of bath oil or something in there that you might like."

"But it's not mine."

"I know. Jenny said she got it for overnight guests. You pour it into the water and it makes your skin softer."

She thanked him and closed the door, turning on the water again. Just this once, she would fill the tub. While the water rose, she found the bottle of oil. After reading the directions, she poured in the right amount.

To her surprise, bubbles began forming. She stood there watching them, fascinated. She almost forgot to turn off the water before it came over the side of the tub. She removed her clothes and slid into the deliciously warm water.

Heaven! She didn't think she would ever get out.

When the pizza came, Joe realized he hadn't heard Ginger moving around. He knocked on the bedroom door to let her know their late dinner had arrived. No answer.

Slowly he opened the bedroom door, expecting to see her sound asleep on the bed. But the room was empty. He moved to the bathroom and listened at the door. Complete silence. "Ginger?" he called softly.

There was no response.

He was afraid he'd scare her if he opened the door. After all, he'd told her she'd have her privacy. But worry gripped him. Slowly he turned the knob and pushed back the door.

His princess was asleep in the bath, her auburn hair resting on the back of the tub, bubbles covering everything but her face. Despite how beautiful she looked, he realized the danger in the situation. She might have drowned.

He started to wake her up, but he realized she'd be embarrassed. Instead, he backed out of the room and closed the door behind him. Then he banged on the door from the bedroom and shouted her name.

There was a large splash. "W-what? What is it?"

"I just wanted to let you know the pizza's here. I don't want it to get cold."

"I'll be right— I don't have a robe."

"I'll put one on your bed. Just give me a minute."

He had a terry-cloth robe his mother had given him for Christmas that he hadn't used. He put it on the bed, lingering a minute to imagine his robe sliding over Ginger's skin.

The bathroom door opened slightly, and he said, "It's here. I'll go back to the kitchen. You want something to drink? I have some caffeine-free cola so you can get to sleep tonight. Is that okay?''

"Yes, please."

Reluctantly he left the bedroom and waited for his wife to join him in the kitchen. It would be their first meal at home together.

Four

Joe rolled over in his big bed and slowly opened his eyes. He normally rose early each morning, but he'd stayed up last night, lingering over the pizza with Ginger. Too late, actually. Ginger should have been in bed several hours earlier. But she'd seemed to enjoy the late-night snack and his company.

They'd compared childhoods, hers in difficult circumstances in Estonia, with little to eat and almost no money. She was an only child of a single woman, shunned by many of the people in their town. Her mother had decided to marry an American. She was only thirty-four now, having had Ginger at fifteen.

Joe hadn't really thought about his family and his younger days when he and his brothers had played and laughed together. His heart-breaking romance with his fiancée seemed silly now. He had a loving, supportive family, a good education, a profession he enjoyed. He had nothing to complain about. He was glad he'd decided to help Ginger. She deserved to stay in America.

He grinned and swung back the cover. They had a lot to do today. He wanted to get her things out of that one-room apartment she had called home. They had to go to the jewelry store to pick out some diamonds to go with her wedding band. He wanted to introduce Ginger to his friends. He needed to go to the closest INS office and give them a copy of their marriage certificate.

He also wanted to buy Ginger a dress for the opening of the Men's Grill. As the architect's wife, she'd be in the spotlight.

His life was suddenly much more exciting than it had been on Friday.

Fifteen minutes later, he came out of his room, following the scent of bacon and coffee. He expected to see Ginger, of course, but he was hungry, too. He was glad she felt at home enough to cook this morning. Not that he expected her to cook every meal, but it was a good way to start.

Ginger wasn't in the kitchen. There was a note on the counter that made him frown.

Joe,
I have to be at work and it takes me a while to walk from here. Your breakfast is keeping warm in the oven. I made you a sandwich for lunch. It's in the refrigerator. There's also a casserole in the refrigerator for your dinner. I work until six-thirty and my class starts at seven. I will be home by ten-thirty. Leave the dishes for me. I'll finish the laundry tonight. I dusted the furniture but did not vacuum because I didn't want to wake you.

Thank you.
Ginger

He looked at the clock on the kitchen wall. It was only nine-fifteen and she'd already done all that work? That was more than most people did in a full day. Not to mention she intended to be on her feet until six-thirty and go to school after that.

He grabbed his car keys. Then he went back and opened the oven to find a plate of scrambled eyes, bacon and toast there. He made a quick sandwich with it and hurried out to his car.

He'd hoped he'd find Ginger on the street and could pick her up, but he didn't see her anywhere. He parked in the lot of the Lone Star Country Club and hurried into the building.

Harvey Small was entering his office when he caught sight of Joe.

"Joe, I was going to call you. I have some questions about the opening. Come right in."

"No. I need to find Ginger."

"She's working. Now, about the flowers we're—"

"Where is she?"

"She's in the Yellow Rose Café, setting up for lunch. Now, about the—"

Joe ignored the man and hurried to the café. There were several waitresses setting the tables, but he didn't see Ginger. Then she came from the kitchen, carrying a tray of salt, pepper and ketchup for the tables.

"Ginger!" he exclaimed.

She stopped and carefully set the tray on the nearest table. "Yes, Mr. Turner?"

He couldn't believe she was calling him Mr. Turner. "What did you say?"

"I asked what you wanted."

"It was the 'Mr. Turner' bit that bothered me," he growled.

"Joe, I was talking to you," Harvey called from the door, moving toward them.

"I know, but I need to talk to my wife." It was Ginger's reaction that had him turning to stare at Harvey, who appeared stunned.

Then he managed a small laugh. "Come on, Joe, if you want a cup of coffee before we talk, just say so." He turned to Ginger. "Get Mr. Turner some coffee and bring it to my office. And maybe a Danish, Joe?"

"No. I've had breakfast. My wife fixed it for me."

"What are you talking about? I know you're not married, Joe. Your mother complains about it all the time. Now, what I needed—"

"Meet Ginger Turner, my wife." While Joe said those magical words, he slid his arm around Ginger's waist.

Harvey stared at them as if he'd seen a ghost. "Ginger…Ginger is your wife?"

"Yes, we got married on Saturday. I'll need to talk to you about her hours."

"No, Joe, you mustn't!" Ginger protested.

"Yes, sweetheart, I must. You can't keep the schedule you proposed for today. It's too much."

"But I fixed all your food. I'm sorry the casserole

is not very good, but you didn't have much food in your refrigerator.''

"Ginger, I'm not complaining about the food. I'm complaining about how much you're trying to do.''

It frustrated Joe that she didn't seem to comprehend his concern.

It was Ginger who spoke next. "Mr. Small, if you will excuse me for five minutes, I need to talk to Joe, er, Mr. Turner, and then I will return to work.''

Joe hated her kowtowing to Harvey. "We'll take as long as we need, Ginger. Harvey doesn't mind, do you, Harvey?'' He shot the club manager a determined look as he took Ginger's arm and led her through the doors into the Men's Grill.

"Joe, Mr. Small will be mad at me. He may dock my wages,'' Ginger said with fear.

"I'll bet he doesn't,'' Joe said grimly.

"But what's wrong? I'm only doing what you said,'' Ginger said, a plea in her voice.

"What are you talking about? I never said for you to work yourself into the ground. And walking to work from the condo? That's ridiculous.''

"But I had to get to work.''

"That's just it. You *don't* have to come to work.''

She stared at him, panic in her eyes. "You said I could continue to work, to save my money if they send me back.''

"Honey, I said you could work, but not all the time. You're taking nine hours a week at the community college and working every other minute here. You need more time to relax. I'm going to tell Harvey to cut you back to…to twenty hours a week. Okay?''

"No!" Ginger cried, tears in her eyes. "You promised."

She had him there. He had promised, but he'd had no idea how many hours she put in. "How many do you usually work?"

She ducked her head. "Sixty to seventy hours a week."

"Good Lord, that's slavery!"

"No. He pays me and I get tips, too. Please?''

"Do they feed you lunch today?" He'd decided to gather his arguments and renegotiate their terms when they had privacy and more time.

"Yes, of course. And…and I will try to get more done tomorrow."

He shook his head and then pulled her into his arms for a kiss that he had to have. "I'll be here at six-thirty to drive you to school."

"Oh, no, that's not necessary. I can—"

He kissed her again. "If you're going to work the rest of the day and go to school, you have no choice, Ginger. My wife will not be walking the streets at night. Understand?" His voice was fierce, and she slowly nodded, watching him with a careful eye. He kissed her gently this time, then he strode out of the room.

Ginger slipped back into the café and picked up her tray. As soon as the other waitresses noticed her return, they hurried over to ask her questions.

Erica Clawson, one of the waitresses Ginger didn't like, asked, "Did you really catch Joe Turner? I'm impressed."

Ginger stared at her blankly.

"Leave her alone, Erica," Daisy Parker, her best friend and fellow waitress, warned. "Ginger is a wonderful person. Joe Turner is lucky if she married him."

"Well, someone certainly is," Erica returned. "I've heard he's loaded. If I didn't want my guy, I would've gone after Joe."

Ginger bit her bottom lip. It was tempting to say Joe was hers, but she knew he really wasn't.

"We never see you with your guy," another waitress said. "I'm beginning to wonder if he's real."

Her words didn't faze Erica. "Oh, he's real, all right. Look at this." She reached in the neckline of her blouse and pulled out a gold chain with a large diamond hanging from it. "See what he gave me?"

After looking at Erica's necklace, the women, almost in unison, looked at Ginger's left hand.

"That's a lovely band," Daisy said, smiling at Ginger.

"Yeah," Erica said, syrup dripping from her voice. "You can find a lot of them at the drug store."

Harvey opened the door, and the waitresses scattered to do their jobs. Daisy squeezed Ginger's hand before she hurried to the kitchen.

Harvey came over to Ginger. "Did he really marry you?"

She nodded, staring down at the table.

"Are you going to quit working for me?"

She shook her head no. "He promised me I could keep working."

"You *want* to keep working? Well, okay, then. That's good." He smiled brilliantly at her and headed back to his office.

Ginger knew why Harvey wanted her to continue to work. She never complained about working long hours and she always came in when he asked. She had been grateful for the opportunity to earn more money.

When the lunch crowds began to come into the café, the tables were properly set and everything was spic and span. Ginger smiled and greeted her customers, efficiently taking orders, just like any other day, until Amy, with her three children and Mrs. Turner, Joe's mother, entered.

The hostess seated them at the last of Ginger's tables. As she turned to go, she stopped by Ginger and whispered, "These people asked for your section."

Ginger continued serving meals at the table two rows over, but she peeked in their direction and found Joe's family smiling and waving to her.

She hurried over. "Hello."

"Do you mind that we asked for you?" Vivian Turner asked.

"Of course not, Mrs. Turner. What would you like to eat today?" She nodded to the children, Robbie, Drew and Katie. "I bet you want hamburgers with French fries. Am I right?"

The three children nodded and Ginger looked at Amy for approval. The two ladies made their choices. As Ginger turned to go to the kitchen, she heard a familiar voice. "No, I need to sit in Ginger's section."

Joe had come back to the café for lunch. Had he not liked the sandwich she'd made for him?

"But, sir, all her tables are full."

"She's my wife and I'm sitting in her section."

He was going to announce their marriage to everyone in Mission Creek if she didn't do something. Ginger hurried over to the hostess and whispered that she would take care of him. Then she took him by the hand and led him to his mother's table. "You can sit here with Robbie, Joe. Robbie, will you keep an eye on your uncle for me?" she asked with a teasing smile for the little boy.

Robbie, eight, giggled, and nodded.

Before he sat down, Joe leaned over and kissed her briefly. Ginger was horrified at his behavior, but he sat down as if nothing unusual had happened.

"I'll have a club sandwich, sweetheart. Okay?"

"Yes, of course, Mr. Turner." Then she hurried away.

"I think you embarrassed her," Amy whispered to Joe.

"Yeah. She thinks she still has to call me Mr. Turner, even though we're married."

His mother frowned at him. "Everyone doesn't know you're married. There'd probably be some complaints about her behavior and she'd be reprimanded.''

"She'd better not be," Joe said grimly. "After all, she didn't kiss me. I kissed her." He reminded himself to stop by Harvey's office and be sure Ginger wasn't punished for his behavior.

"Mom, I need to talk to you." He waited until his mother switched her attention from her grandchildren to him. "I need some advice."

His sister-in-law Amy grinned. "Trouble in paradise already?"

Amy was a sweet woman, but she loved to tease. While that made her a good fit for their family, this time Joe didn't appreciate her sense of humor. "Of course not! I mean, well, I don't know what to do."

His mother raised an eyebrow and smiled at Amy before turning to Joe. "Don't you think you should have this conversation with your father?"

He started to get up and walk away, but that wouldn't fix his problem. "Look, I'm serious." He told them Ginger's schedule for the day, and Amy stared at him.

"You're kidding. She *walked* to work this morning? And fixed meals for all day for you? And she's going to school tonight?"

"Well," Mrs. Turner said, "no one will ever accuse your wife of being lazy."

"I came after her and tried to convince her to come home with me, but she begged me to let her stay. Her eyes were full of tears." He shrugged his shoulders. "I didn't know what to do."

Amy grinned again. "I know you're going to fuss at me, but Bill would tell you to count your blessings."

"No, he wouldn't," Joe returned. "He's always bragging about how hard you work."

"But I don't work that much. Your wife's a dynamo."

"I thought I was going to give her a better life, an easier life, but all I've done is make her work harder. Mom, can't you tell her that she can't work this hard, that she should let me take care of her? I think all the boys' teasing about me not having any money upset her."

Ginger came back to their table, holding a big tray overhead. She set up a tray holder, then began delivering their food, the children's first.

"Ginger, that was very fast," Vivian said with a smile.

"Thank you. Pedro is the chef today and he's very good."

Amy leaned forward. "I don't see how you lift such a big tray. Isn't it heavy?"

"No, no, it's not heavy. Besides, I'm used to it."

"I don't suppose you can sit with us?" Joe asked, sure he already knew the answer.

"No," she said, not smiling.

"I'll be back here to pick you up at six-thirty, okay?"

She ducked her head, but she nodded before hurrying away.

"Well? Any ideas?"

Mrs. Turner frowned, but Amy suggested, "Whenever Bill wants me to agree to something, he waits until after we make love and I'm almost asleep. He figures I won't have much resistance then."

"I think that's unfair of Bill," Vivian said. "But pillow talk usually does work as long as it's something for her own good. Try that, dear."

Great! The one thing he couldn't do was what they suggested. He'd have to try to talk to her when he got her home from school.

He'd already decided he was going to get her a car to simplify her life. He'd take care of that this afternoon. He'd already purchased a diamond ring for her, which he'd thought he'd give to her today at lunch, so eager was he to let everyone know about their marriage.

But he'd changed his mind. He'd give it to her tonight at home. Too bad he couldn't give it to her during pillow talk, as his mother had called it. He was beginning to find some things about this marriage that were decidedly inconvenient.

At six-twenty-five that evening, Joe parked in the side parking lot, near the door the hired help used. He'd been busy all day. He'd talked to the INS agents, telling them that he and Ginger were now married, and faxed them the marriage certificate. They told him he wouldn't need to visit them. They'd be in contact when they were ready for an interview.

Then he'd talked to the apartment manager where Ginger had lived. He couldn't get the man to return the rent she'd paid for the rest of the month, so she'd have plenty of time to decide what to do with the sofa and table and chairs.

Last, but not least, he'd bought a car for Ginger. Now she wouldn't have to ride the bus or walk everywhere. He'd chosen a secondhand Honda Accord. He wasn't sure how well she drove and he thought he'd get this one for her to practice on. It was supposed to be safe and easy to handle.

At six-thirty, she stepped out into the late sunshine. He saw her pale face and knew she was exhausted. He got out of the car and hurried to give her a hug. "Hi, honey. Are you doing okay? Sure you want to go to school? You could skip class tonight." Then he'd have time to talk to her.

"No, I can't do that. The math professor is going over the test we are taking next week," Ginger said.

He hugged her close before he stood back. "Okay, if you insist. Did you eat dinner?"

"No, there wasn't time. We were very crowded tonight."

"Honey, you've got to have some dinner before you go to school. I know, we'll stop by the condo and get that sandwich you made for my lunch today. It looks good. I didn't eat it because I wanted to see you."

"Are you sure you don't want it?"

He smiled for the first time, glad to see some interest in her beautiful eyes. He led her to the car.

"This is not your car," she protested.

"It is now."

"You got rid of your beautiful car?"

"You don't like this one?" Had he made a mistake?

"No, this is a fine car, but your other car was wonderful, too. I just wondered why you would make a change."

"I didn't," he assured her. "I bought this one for you, so you can get to school and back safely. You can drive it tonight."

She gasped, her eyes as big as saucers as she stared at him. "No, I can't. There's a bus that stops by my apartment. I'll go there and catch the bus."

"No, you won't. If you want to wait until you get used to driving it, that's fine. But you're going to school by car tonight. One of us will be driving."

"It will not be me," she said quietly, and leaned her head against the headrest.

"Honey, you're just being plain stubborn about this. It's the husband's job to keep you safe, to provide for you."

"But when I tried to do what a wife is supposed to do, you complained about it."

"What are you talking about?" he asked, staring at her.

"You said the wife's job was to cook and clean. I cooked all the meals this morning. I started your laundry and will finish it this evening. I'll find time to buy the groceries tomorrow and I'll iron the shirts, but maybe not until tomorrow evening, if you don't mind."

"You're doing all this because you thought I expected it? Lord have mercy, I wanted to make your life easier, not harder. You're trying to do too much.''

"No. I'm trying to do my share." Her lips tightened, she crossed her arms over her chest and stared straight ahead.

Joe rubbed the back of his neck. "I didn't mean— Look, honey, when wives go to school at night and work full-time and— Well, that's too much. I have a maid who comes in and cleans once a week, and my shirts go to the cleaners every week. Your cooking is great when you have time to eat it with me. You don't have school on Wednesday night, right?"

"Yes," she said quietly, as if she dreaded his response.

"Okay, we'll cook dinner Wednesday." He started the car and backed out, assuming everything was settled.

"No."

He couldn't believe it. "Why not?"

"Because I work late on Wednesday nights."

He heaved a sigh. "We've got to talk about your schedule."

He looked at her tired, unhappy face. "But not tonight." He drew a deep breath. "Now, I want you to watch me handle the car. When we get to the stop sign, you can get behind the wheel."

"No. I don't know how to drive."

Five

Joe took Ginger to school, letting her out with a warning to meet him there after class. Then he went home to figure out what to do.

When he picked her up at ten o'clock, he still didn't have an answer.

"Did you get a look at the test?" he asked, as if he was only concerned with her grades.

"Not the test, exactly, but he told us some possible questions. But I already knew those things."

"Good, so you don't need to study tonight." He was determined to settle things this evening. He was too frustrated to let things continue.

"Not for that class. But I have that history test tomorrow. It's mid-semester, you know." She leaned back in her seat and closed her eyes.

"That's why we've got to talk tonight."

She raised her head and stared at him as he pulled onto the road. "What are you saying?"

"I'm saying we have to talk. You can't work as many hours as you have in the past."

"You promised!" She drew a deep breath. "I explained why. I need as much money as I can save in the event I have to return to Estonia."

"You're not going to Estonia. You're staying right here in the U.S., as my wife, for at least a year."

"I can't. Those men won't let me." She turned her face away from him and leaned her forehead against the window. The temptation to pull to the side of the road and comfort her was strong. But he didn't. Instead Joe sped up, anxious to get her inside before they had their argument.

And he was determined to have an argument. He had promised she could continue to work, but he'd had no idea she meant to work seventy hours a week.

After they entered the condo, he nodded toward the kitchen table. "Go sit down. I'm going to get us both a bowl of ice cream for a snack."

"But I have to finish the laundry. It needs to go in the dryer so I can fold it before I go to bed." She started toward the utility room.

Joe caught her by the arm. "No. Not yet. We're going to come to some decisions."

She pulled away from him, but he pointed at the table and she slowly sat down. "I don't understand what's wrong."

"I'm going to explain." He took out a couple of bowls and got the ice cream from the freezer. "I went to the grocery store tonight, but I only bought a few things. Ice cream was one of them. I hope you like cookies 'n' cream."

She watched him but didn't answer. He looked at her, but he didn't try to coax a smile from her.

When he put her bowl in front of her, she didn't pick up the spoon he'd provided.

"You'd better eat it before it melts."

She ignored the ice cream and continued to stare at him.

"Ginger, I know you're tired. But I'm trying to make it easier on you. Eat a little, please?" He gave her his best smile. He figured she'd prefer charm to him taking her in his arms. That was getting to be too easy—and too pleasant.

She picked up the spoon and took a bite. Then she looked at him. "What is it? Are you tired of being married to me? Do you want me to go?"

"No, of course not." He took a spoonful of ice cream, too. "I just think we need to change a few things. When I said you could work, I didn't mean you could work so many hours. It's impossible to work that much, still go to school and be my wife at the same time."

"I can manage."

"When will I have time to teach you to drive?"

"I don't need to drive. I'll learn the other bus routes so I can get to school and home. I mean, here."

"My family, and half the town, won't believe we're married if I let you do that."

"Why not?" she asked, a confused look on her face.

"Because my friends don't ride the bus." He knew that was a dumb reason, but he had to start somewhere. "Remember you were worried about me sacrificing myself by marrying you and I said it would help me, that it would stop my family from trying to set me up with different women?''

She nodded, but she was frowning.

"Well, it won't help at all unless we act like married people."

"Married people ride the bus all the time!" she exclaimed.

He sighed. "I know they do, honey, but my friends don't. They'll know something is wrong if I let you ride the bus."

"Then I will walk."

"That's too dangerous, especially at night. Haven't you ever been scared doing that?"

He hadn't expected her to admit anything, but she slowly nodded, avoiding his gaze.

"What? When?"

She bit her bottom lip, then said, "It was before. And he let me go."

"You know who it was? Did you report him to the police? Did he hurt you?" Joe felt his heart beat faster at the thought of someone hurting Ginger. "What did he do to you?"

She only shook her head, not looking at him.

"Ginger, did he hurt you?"

"No, he didn't. I—I told him what he wanted to know."

Joe frowned. Her answer didn't make any sense. "What are you talking about?"

Tears began running down Ginger's pale cheeks. "I betrayed my friend. I wasn't brave enough."

He actually felt jealousy rise in him. "What friend?"

"Don't make me tell you, Joe, please? I promised myself I would never do that again, even if he used the knife."

Joe stood and came around the table, pulling Ginger from her chair into his arms. "Honey, don't cry. Was your friend Daisy?" He'd suddenly remembered her talking about the other waitress, Daisy, calling her her best friend.

She began shaking, and the tears turned into sobs as she nodded.

He drew a deep breath and pressed her closer to him. "Someone threatened you with a knife to force you to reveal a secret about Daisy?"

With her head pressed into his chest, she nodded.

He couldn't imagine a secret about Daisy that would be that important, but he didn't really care. Ginger was his concern.

"You didn't have a choice, honey. I'm sure Daisy would understand that. Where did this happen?"

"When I started home one night, he was in the parking lot at the club. He grabbed me."

"I think we need more lights in that parking lot. I'll see to it. But that's why you're not going to walk the streets at night. Or the daytime, either. I'm going to teach you to drive." He waited for her response, but she said nothing. After kissing her forehead, he eased her back down into her chair.

"Eat some more ice cream." He sat back down in his chair, too. "You see, Ginger, if I was truly married, I'd protect my wife, just like I want to protect you. And you're not going to be sent back to Estonia. We're married, and we'll stay married for at least a year. Then, when we separate, I'll give you money to help you manage.''

''No! You're giving me a chance to stay here. I can't take your money.''

He should have known she would respond that way. ''Okay, then, will you help me? Will you pretend like we're married? I have money, Ginger. I'm going to have to spend some on you. But more important, I'm going to have to spend time with you, or no one will believe we're married.''

''But how can I—''

''By working a lot less at the club. I can't ask you to give up your school. You'd lose all the hours you've gone to class and studied. But I'll provide the money if you'll give me some time. For example, when they have the opening of the Men's Grill Saturday night, I'll need you by my side, not working. And I'll need you dressed in a cocktail dress.''

She opened her mouth to protest, but he raised his hand. ''My friends will expect it.''

''Your friends seem very demanding,'' she grumbled, which brought a grin to his face.

''Yeah, they are. Remember, I grew up here. They know me well.''

''So I must ask Harvey to take Saturday night off? He won't like it.''

''Not just Saturday night. I don't want you working at night anymore. We'll need time to do some shopping and driving lessons. Mom is already talking about a big party to celebrate our marriage. I haven't even told my godfather yet. He'll probably want to give us a party, too."

"Who is your godfather?"

"Archy Wainwright." He grinned when her eyes widened in surprise. "He and Dad are best friends."

"But the Wainwrights and the Carsons started the club!"

"Oh, yeah. And you can bet they'll all be there Saturday night. Now, I know you're tired and you need to get some rest. I'll drive you to the club in the morning and change your schedule with Harvey. You can work five days a week, but not longer than nine-thirty to two. That will give us some afternoons to spend together, and the nights you don't have school."

"But I won't make much money."

"True, but I'm going to give you money to do things. You can save every penny you make. Go get ready for bed."

"But the laundry—"

"The maid comes tomorrow. Do you want her to have nothing to do? Trust me, sweetheart. Everything will get taken care of."

To his relief, Ginger nodded and went to her room. He'd convinced her more easily than he'd thought—mainly because she believed she owed him for marrying her.

He was beginning to think it might be him who

owed her. Life was a lot more fun now that Ginger was with him.

The next morning Joe got up at his normal time, seven. He slipped into some jeans and a T-shirt and headed for the kitchen, where he found Ginger making a pot of coffee.

"Good morning. I thought maybe you'd sleep in today."

"I'm used to getting up early," Ginger told him. "I think we still have a few eggs and some bacon. Is that okay for breakfast?"

"Of course it is. But it's my turn to cook for you."

"You said the wife does the cooking."

"Damn, I wish I'd never opened my mouth. You always remember what I said." From what his friends told him, their wives never remembered anything they said. Not true of Ginger.

She smiled at him, relieving his mind. He was afraid he'd upset her last night. "You may make the toast."

"It's a deal," he said. "And after you get off work this afternoon, we'll do some grocery shopping. Then we'll come home and you can study."

"You won't mind?" she asked.

As he answered, she moved to the refrigerator to take out the essentials for breakfast. "Not at all. What period are you studying?"

"The Civil War. It was a terrible time."

"Yes, it was. We don't fight ourselves anymore, except for gangs, drug wars, things like that." He hadn't thought of those things as war, but he guessed they were.

"There is crime in Estonia, too."

"Uh, yeah. But you're not going there again. Hand out the butter. I think I'll broil the toast, since we have time. I like it that way."

Once everything was ready, they sat together and had a leisurely breakfast.

"I like starting my day like this," he told her with a smile.

"But what about work?"

"Right now I'm finishing up a few little details at the club. But I'm thinking about starting my own architectural firm here in Mission Creek." For months that idea had been floating around in his mind, but last night, knowing he'd need to stay here in Mission Creek for at least a year for Ginger's sake, he'd finally made the decision.

"You won't have to go to a big city to find work?"

"Were you worried about that?" he asked, seeing the frown on her face.

"Maybe. I don't want to leave Mission Creek. But you were living in Chicago, you said. I was afraid— I mean, you might want to go back."

Joe smiled. "I thought I would, but now I don't think so. I've enjoyed being back home with my family."

"They are very nice."

"Yeah, if they don't tease you to death. I've got to go shave and shower before it's time to go. It's only eight-thirty, but I'd better get started. Let's stack the dishes in the sink and leave them to the maid. She should be—'' The doorbell rang.

"She's here." He hurried to the door. "Come in, Maria. I want to introduce you to my wife." He led the way to the kitchen. Then he realized what he'd forgotten. "Uh, Maria, I got married this past weekend. This is my wife, Ginger."

He hurriedly got down a cup and poured some coffee for Maria.

"Oh, no, Mr. Turner. I need to start work." Maria nodded to Ginger, but she didn't sit down.

"Uh, I need you to explain to Ginger what you do. She may have some other chores for you. In fact, I wondered if you could spare me another day. Maybe Friday as well as Tuesday?"

"Yes, I guess I can. Mrs. Wilson doesn't need me anymore."

"Perfect, Maria. Talk to Ginger about what you do." He leaned over and kissed Ginger before he slipped out of the kitchen.

Instead of heading for his shower, he went instead to Ginger's bedroom. It hadn't occurred to him that they couldn't let Maria see that they weren't sharing a room. He opened the drawers and closet and scooped up the few clothes Ginger had put in there and hurried back to his room. He was making a second trip when Ginger ran into him.

"What's Maria doing?" he demanded in a whisper.

"She's cleaning the kitchen. But, Joe, you don't

have to pay her to do what I should do.'' Ginger finally noticed that he was carrying her books for school. ''What are you doing?''

''I'm putting all your things in my room. Maria mustn't know we aren't, uh, sharing the same room.''

''She will tell?''

''I can't ask her to lie for us. That wouldn't be fair.''

''But why would they ask her?''

''Because they will think she'll know. Go gather up what's left and bring the towel you used.''

Ginger felt strange going into Joe's room. Not only was his bedroom bigger than the entire apartment she and her mother had shared in Estonia, but Joe wasn't in sight.

Then she realized the door to his private bath was closed and she could hear the shower running. She almost stopped breathing as she pictured him with water sluicing down his broad chest.

Unlike most of the men at the club, he didn't play golf. His favorite exercise, she recalled, was racquetball. Once she had brought a pot of coffee to some men waiting for a court. Joe had been playing and she'd paused to watch him. He was fast and strong.

She shook her head as if to dispel the memory, then remembered why she was in here. Purposefully she opened the walk-in closet, found some space on several shelves and put her personal items there.

Then she headed for the kitchen, thinking it best to give Joe some privacy.

But when she went into the kitchen, she discovered Maria had already washed the dishes. "Oh!"

"What is the matter, señora?"

"I—I was going to have a little more coffee, but—"

"Of course, señora," Maria said, reaching for a clean cup. "I will pour it for you."

"No. I don't want to make more work for you."

Maria gave her a curious look. "It is my job." Then she poured the coffee. "Do you want to drink it while you watch the news?"

"The news?" Ginger asked. She didn't own a television and had never made a habit of watching it. But she didn't want to disagree with Maria. She was already causing her extra work. "Yes, please, that will be fine."

"Does señor want more coffee?"

"No, he's in the shower."

Maria walked past her, carrying her cup of coffee, and Ginger followed her. Maria clicked on the television, then set the coffee on the coffee table and went back to the kitchen.

Ginger stood there, uncertain what to do. She couldn't go back into the kitchen and bother Maria. She couldn't go into Joe's bedroom and disturb him. And she no longer had her own bedroom.

Would she sleep on the sofa tonight? Or perhaps she could slip into the bedroom she'd been using after Maria left. If not, what was she going to do?

Her knees felt weak at that thought. She sank down to the sofa and picked up the coffee cup. That was what she would do. She could get her clothing for the next day each evening and sleep in the same bed she'd been using. But before Maria came, she would strip the bed and put everything in Joe's room.

Surely Joe would want that. It would take time, but she wasn't going to work as much. She could handle a little extra effort. Was it possible, as Joe had said, that she would be able to stay here for a year? Maybe stay in Mission Creek for years without having to worry about being returned to Estonia? Or to her mother?

Should she call her mother and let her know that her daughter was now married and beyond that evil man's reach? Would it help her mother?

It was the first time contacting her mother had occurred to Ginger. She knew the number by memory. After a quick look at Joe's closed door, she picked up the phone from the lamp table. Dialing the number, she tensely waited for someone to answer, hopefully her mother.

"Hello?"

"Mama, it is Virvela," she said softly.

"Where are you?"

"I can't tell you, but I want you to know I am married. I'm not coming back."

"You must! They will beat me again."

"I'm married, Mama. He can't marry me."

"He didn't want to marry you. I am the one who insisted on marriage. I did that for you!"

"Well, I'm not coming back. Goodbye, Mama."

Her mother was scolding her in her native tongue as Ginger hung up. She didn't even realize she was crying until Joe came out of his room and approached her.

"Ginger? What's wrong? Why are you crying? Did Maria say something mean?"

"No. Maria was wonderful. I—I'm sorry. I know I should've asked but I called Mama. I told her I was married and would not be coming back."

"She was unhappy?"

"She said they would beat her again. She said the man did not want to marry me, that she insisted he do so."

Joe reached over and wiped her cheeks. "It doesn't matter what he wanted, sweetheart. He can't mess with you now. You belong to me."

"I don't want to cause you trouble." She wiped the new tears away. "What if—"

"No. You're safe. They don't know where you are. But don't call her again, okay? At least not before we talk about it."

"Yes, I'm sorry."

"Come on. We're going to talk to Harvey now. We'll fight one battle at a time, okay?"

She nodded but couldn't stop the tears from rolling down her cheeks.

He pulled her against him. "If you keep crying, everyone will think I'm being mean to my wife." She looked up to protest and Joe kissed her. "You know, you have the softest lips, Mrs. Turner. And your husband sure does enjoy kissing you. Good thing it's part of the job.''

"But no one can see us now. There's no need—''

Maria appeared at the door as if on cue. She smiled when she saw Joe's arms around Ginger.

"Oh, hi, Maria," Joe said with a grin. "We're just leaving."

"Sí, señor."

He turned Ginger around and led her to the door, her hand snug in his. Ginger didn't protest. For once she felt safe and secure.

Six

Harvey greeted Ginger with a smile, but his smile didn't extend to Joe. "What are you doing here, Joe? Are you finally going to discuss the opening with me?"

"No, Harvey, I'm here to discuss my wife's schedule with you."

Harvey immediately looked at Ginger. "You told me you wanted to continue working. Tell him."

Joe sat back and looked at Ginger. He could tell she was sympathetic to Harvey. He hoped she kept her word to him.

"Mr. Small, I didn't realize how much time it would take to...to be Joe's wife. I can't work as many hours. I'm very sorry."

"So you want Sundays off?"

Ginger sank her teeth into her bottom lip and looked at Joe. He knew what she wanted. "No, Harvey," he said calmly. "She's cutting back to about twenty hours a week."

"What? You can't do that! I'll be shorthanded. That's impossible." Harvey straightened his shoulders and stared at Joe, as if daring him to do such a thing.

"My wife has no need to work at all, Harvey. You know that. So it's your choice. Some or none."

"Ginger," Harvey began, pleading in his tone, "if you cut back so many hours, I won't have anyone to fill in. It will be difficult—"

Joe leaned over and kissed Ginger's lips as she started to speak. "Honey, you'd best go get started or you'll be late. I'll finish the conversation with Harvey."

Ginger looked at her watch. "Oh! I didn't realize it was so late. Sorry, Mr. Small." She hurried from the office.

"You did that on purpose!" Harvey accused, staring at Joe.

"Yes, I did. You've been letting her work too much ever since she started here. If I were you, I'd accept the decision. Otherwise, I'll convince Ginger to quit altogether and your management practices will receive much closer scrutiny from the club president."

With a deep frown, Harvey nodded, which made Joe wonder what else he was doing that was against the rules. Standing to leave, Joe remembered something else. "I'm going to look at the employee parking lot. I've heard the lighting isn't good."

"It wasn't part of the redo. There's as much lighting as there ever was."

"Yeah. I'll let you know what I find."

Then he walked out.

While they prepared the Yellow Rose Café for lunch, Ginger told Daisy about her change of schedule.

"I'm so glad, Ginger. You were working too much."

"But I—I didn't tell you about the INS because I didn't want you to get in trouble. I'm not a citizen. I was saving money for when I was sent back to Estonia."

"But now that you've married Joe, you won't be sent back. That's terrific!"

Ginger wasn't ready to celebrate. "We have to pass a test."

"What kind of test?" Daisy asked. "Like the one in that movie about getting a green card? I rented the video a couple of months ago. It wasn't hard. They asked personal questions, that's all. If your marriage is real, it won't be hard."

Ginger smiled, as if she hadn't a care in the world, while she frantically thought of all she didn't know about her husband. She would never pass such a test. In spite of Joe's promise, she realized again that she could be sent back in three months.

When two o'clock rolled around, it seemed very strange to walk out of the club. Joe was there waiting for her in the parking lot.

"Ready to do some shopping?" he asked, smiling at her.

"Yes, of course." That was why he had told her she needed to get off early. And she could study for her test after the grocery shopping.

They started down the long drive to the main highway. "By the way," Joe said, "we're going to install more lights in that back parking lot."

"That's good," she agreed. She tried to avoid thinking about the attack on her, when she thought she was going to die. The realization that she wouldn't be working nights, which meant she wouldn't have to get home in the dark, felt good.

In the grocery store, Joe pushed the cart and told her to put in whatever she wanted to cook.

"For tonight?"

"For three or four days, at least."

She bought a lot of pasta, some peanut butter and crackers, two cans of tuna fish and one box of microwave popcorn after some hesitation. "Is this all right? I always wanted to try this."

"Of course it's all right. What else?"

She added some fresh vegetables so she could make sauce for the pasta. Then she stopped. "That's all."

Joe grinned at her. "Sweetheart, I don't mean to complain, but I like steak. And we'll need eggs and bacon for breakfast, bread and ham for sandwiches. For dessert, maybe a cake, more ice cream. Can you make peach cobbler?"

"Yes, I think so," she said hesitantly. "But that will all be expensive."

"I know, but I need a lot of food to keep me going. I'm not little like you."

They made another tour of the store and filled the cart. While Ginger delighted in such freedom to buy so much, she began to worry about eating it all.

Together they unpacked the groceries when they got home. Ginger discovered doing chores together was a lot of fun, though a little slower than doing it alone. But she enjoyed herself. She immediately opened the cake mix to make dessert. Then she planned dinner itself.

Joe had some things to do and left her to her planning. He began pulling out some papers from his briefcase. After weeks of not knowing what he wanted to do—return to Chicago or stay in Mission Creek—he'd made up his mind. He was staying there as long as Ginger needed him. He'd promised.

Which meant he needed to open his own office. While he'd thought about his future, he'd surveyed the business spaces available in Mission Creek.

He was studying the brochure for the site he'd chosen when the phone rang. He picked up the receiver and said, "Joe Turner."

Silence.

He hung up the phone after trying to find out if anyone was there.

The phone rang again.

"Joe Turner."

"Is this…Joe Turner from Dallas, Texas?" a female voice asked.

The voice sounded vaguely familiar. "No, I'm sorry. This is Mission Creek, Texas. Are you trying to reach Dallas?"

Before he finished his question, the phone went dead. He stared at it, telling himself it was probably a stranger, though trying to place the voice.

"Joe?" Ginger asked from the kitchen door. "Do you like baked potatoes or mashed?"

"I— Ginger, does your mother's voice sound like yours?"

"Yes, I suppose, except she still has more of an accent."

"Damn!" Joe rubbed his forehead.

"What's the matter?"

"I think that was your mother on the phone. She must have a call display that gave her our number. And now, thanks to me, she knows your husband's name and hometown."

"My mother called? Did she want to talk to me?"

Joe felt even worse than before. He saw the hope in Ginger's eyes. "No, sweetheart. She wanted to know your location. She didn't ask to talk to you."

Ginger stiffened. "No, of course not. How did you say you liked your potatoes?"

"Ginger, will she tell her husband? Will they come here?"

"No, of course not. They don't care about me. And I'm sure his boss wants nothing to do with me since I turned him down. He has a lot of pride." She turned back for the kitchen. "I'll go mash the potatoes."

Joe didn't care about the potatoes, but he did care about Ginger's safety. Later tonight, he'd call his godfather. Perhaps Archy could give Joe some advice.

Ginger served dinner at six. She'd enjoyed her afternoon so much. Meals had always been a necessity to nourish her body, grabbed in a hurry so she could keep going. This evening she'd planned the meal and served it on beautiful china on a lovely table covered by a linen tablecloth. She proudly called Joe to dinner.

"Mmm, something smells good, Ginger. You must be an excellent cook," he said.

Ginger thanked him but denied being a great chef. "It's not difficult to make a good meal when there's money to buy the best food."

"That looks like homemade bread. Did you make it?"

"Yes, of course."

"I am a lucky man."

They began their meal.

"What have you been working on this afternoon?" she asked.

"My new office. If I'm going to stay here, I need an office so I can properly work and attract customers."

"Will you build houses for people?"

"Maybe, but most of my experience is with business facilities. I've heard of several projects they're going to take bids on soon. I'm going to call Archy later on tonight and see what he knows."

"Archy?"

"Archy Wainwright, my godfather. Remember?"

"Yes, but I didn't expect you to call him by his first name. Are people not formal here? At the club, we always call the guests by their surname."

"Yeah, but that's Harvey's doing. By the way, did you study this afternoon?"

"A little, while dinner was cooking."

"I'll clean up so you can do a quick review before class."

She stared at him. "No. That's my job."

"Nowadays, honey, if the husband eats, he should help with either the cooking or the cleaning. I worked while you cooked. Now you'll work while I clean." He grinned as she considered his words, clearly not sure he was telling the truth.

Solemnly, then, he raised his hand as if taking an oath. "I promise, Ginger."

Slowly she said, "That would be nice."

"Good, that's settled."

Once he got Ginger to school, he handed her his cell phone. "I'm going to Archy's for a quick visit. When you finish your test and are ready to go home, press speed dial and then the number seven. Ask for me. Until you see me, don't come out of the building."

"Why?"

"I just want to keep you safe, sweetheart, that's all. We don't want anyone using a knife on you again."

She shuddered before she promised to do as he asked. He felt bad that he had reminded her of the earlier attack, but he thought he had to get her agreement. She was way too independent.

He'd called Archy after he'd finished cleaning the

kitchen, and his godfather had invited Joe over for a drink. Not having talked to him in several weeks, Joe had a few surprises for Archy.

It only took a few minutes to reach the Wainwright ranch, a big, sprawling estate. Archy warmly greeted Joe and invited him into their living room. Justin, his son, was lounging on the sofa, a beer in his hand.

"Justin! I didn't know you'd be here. Good to see you," Joe said with a grin. He and Justin had gone through high school together but had lost touch when Joe went away to school then moved to Chicago. He'd heard about Justin's failed marriage, and he noticed the easy laughter he remembered wasn't there anymore.

"Hi, Joe. Good to see you."

The men shook hands and sat down.

"So, Grandpa," Joe said to Archy with a smile, "how's the newest Wainwright—er, Carson?" Archy had just recently been made a grandfather by the birth of his daughter Rose's son, Wayne Matthew. As much as Archy was delighted to be a grandpa, Joe knew it still galled him that the boy bore the name Carson, which he took from his father, Matt.

Archy's eyes lit up at the mention of the infant. "He's doin' great. A beautiful boy. And I must admit I've never seen Rose look happier, even if the kid's a Carson."

Justin scoffed at the comment, but it was what Joe had expected. Taking it in stride, he went on to say, "Well, I've got some good news myself. I got married last Saturday."

"To whom, boy? And why weren't we invited?" Archy demanded.

Justin quietly said, "Congratulations."

Joe nodded to his old friend, then answered the other two questions. "You weren't invited because we ran away to Vegas, Archy. None of my family was there. And I married Ginger Walton."

Archy frowned, puzzling over the name.

Justin leaned forward. "The pretty redhead at the club, Dad. Your favorite."

"How come you knew who she was?" Archy growled.

"All the men notice her, Dad," Justin said, humor in his voice. Then he turned to Joe. "Now I really mean congratulations, Joe. She's a looker."

"She's more than that," Joe said, struggling to keep his pride in check. "She's a hard worker and a sweet person. She's from Estonia, you know."

Archy shook his head. "Didn't know that." He stared at Joe. "What was wrong with Jenny?"

Joe looked at Archy in surprise. "Is something wrong with Jenny? I thought she was on to another project at the club."

"Of course she is. But I recommended her for the job so you'd get a chance to know her. She's fine-looking and well educated. Might be a better wife than a waitress."

"Dad!" Justin protested. "Don't insult Joe's wife."

"I'm just stating a fact," Archy growled.

Joe had been prepared for Archy's reaction. That

was why he wanted to inform Archy without Ginger present. His godfather had always been blunt. "I can assure you, Archy, Ginger is perfect for me. And while she was working seventy-hour workweeks, she's also been carrying nine hours at the community college."

Justin whistled. "A busy lady."

"Yeah. I feel like I'm taking advantage of her, since I'm so much older than her, but I'm going to take care of her."

Archy started to argue with him, but Joe held up his hand. "I need to talk to you about something before I have to go pick up Ginger from school. Do you still see Johnny Mercado often?"

Archy flashed a look at his son before he turned back to Joe. Johnny was an old friend of his, but he was reputed to be a member of the local mob. Since Justin was the local sheriff, Archy probably didn't want his son to know that he still talked to Johnny. "We have a drink together occasionally. Since his daughter died, Johnny doesn't get out much. Why?"

"Ginger's mother came to America when Ginger was sixteen and married a mob guy in New York City."

"What family?" Justin asked.

"Ginger doesn't know. But her stepfather's boss got a look at Ginger and wanted her. Said he'd marry her." His voice hardened. "He's fifty-eight."

"Johnny wouldn't know anything about a New York mobster," Archy protested.

"Okay." Joe turned to Justin. "I hear you're the

sheriff here now. Did you get a report when a man took a knife to Ginger's throat out at the club?''

Justin sat up straight, his body tense. ''No. I didn't.''

''I didn't think so. By the way, Archy, the club is going to need to erect more lights in the employees parking lot to make it safer.''

Archy frowned, but it was Justin who spoke. ''Why didn't I get a report if it happened?''

''It happened. Ginger didn't report it. She was worried about being deported. She'd run away from home to avoid being forced to marry this old guy in New York.''

''You want to report it now?''

''No, but I'm a little worried. I think Ginger's mother now knows my name and where we live. I wondered if Johnny might hear something, if that family might call in some debts to snatch Ginger.''

Justin wanted details and Joe told him as much as he knew, which really wasn't a lot.

''Are you keeping your eye on her?'' Justin asked.

Archy laughed. ''He's a newlywed, son. Even you should be able to remember those days.''

Joe saw the pain in his friend's eyes and glared at Archy. ''That wasn't necessary, Archy. Yeah, I'm keeping my eye on her. I'm driving her everywhere and then picking her up. I don't know anything else to do.''

''She shouldn't be home alone, either, Joe. She'd answer the door and they'd grab her,'' Justin said.

''Damn, I hadn't thought of that. I was only thinking of danger when she's out of the condo. Good thing I haven't opened my office yet.''

Archy leaned forward. ''You're opening an office?''

''Yeah, I'm staying here. Ginger wants to.''

''Well, at least she accomplished what I wanted Jenny to do. You're back home to stay.''

''Dad, you've got to stop trying to manipulate everyone you know,'' Justin complained. ''Especially your children.''

''Has he been acting up again?'' Joe asked, a half smile on his face. Archy had always expected his children to follow where he led. Though they didn't always, as evidenced by Rose's marriage last year to Matt, the son of his sworn enemy.

''Yeah, as usual.''

The housekeeper entered the living room. ''Mr. Turner, there's a call for you.''

Joe jumped up. ''That will be Ginger calling me to come get her.''

''Bring her back here. I want to get to know her.''

''It's late, Archy. We'll make it another time,'' Joe said as he took the portable phone from the housekeeper. ''Ginger?'' he questioned into the phone.

''Yes, Joe. I'm finished.'' There was a quavery tone to her voice.

''What's wrong, Ginger?''

''There are a couple of men hanging around, watching me,'' she whispered.

''I'll be right there. Stay inside where there are other people.''

"What is it?" Justin asked as Joe handed the housekeeper the phone.

"She thinks two men are following her." Joe ran from the room.

Archy waved Justin in his direction and the sheriff followed Joe.

"Come with me. We'll turn on the sirens," Justin called, and waved Joe in the direction of his official car. In no time they were speeding down the drive.

"Surely it couldn't be her stepfather. He couldn't get here by now." Joe was leaning forward, as if that would help the car go faster.

"Who knows? He may have connected with the Mafia here and hired a couple of goons. Or it might have something to do with that knife-wielding guy at the club. She should've reported it."

"I know," Joe said grimly, not taking his eyes from the road.

It took less than ten minutes to get to the college, but Joe lived and died every one of them. He'd promised Ginger he'd protect her. Then he'd gone blithely off to visit his godfather, leaving her unprotected.

"Quit blaming yourself, Joe. You couldn't expect anything to go wrong so quickly. She's probably all right."

"Do you have your gun with you?"

"Yeah, but I'm sure it won't come to that."

"How long does it take to get a permit?"

"Seven days. But you're not going to need one."

Joe didn't answer. All he could think about was

Ginger's slender body, her fragile appearance. If anyone laid a hand on her, he'd break their neck.

When he saw the college, he drew a deep breath and waved Justin toward the building where he'd let her off. Justin stopped the car in a no-parking zone. Joe jumped out of the car and ran up the steps that led to the door.

He couldn't see Ginger anywhere. The lights were on in the building, but otherwise everything was eerily quiet.

"Do you see her? Was she to meet you here?" Justin called from behind him.

"We didn't specify a place. I told her to stay inside until I got here."

He hoped that was what she'd done. But where was she?

Seven

Joe shoved the door open, yelling Ginger's name as he entered.

Two men were standing in the hall by Ginger's classroom as Joe rounded the corner. One look at him and they ran in the opposite direction.

He would have followed them, except that the ladies' room door opened, slowly at first, then shoved back all the way as Ginger recognized her husband. She flew into his arms, tightly hugging his neck.

Joe had no objection. Feeling her in his arms was a great relief.

"Is she all right?" Justin asked over Joe's shoulder. "Were those two the men she was talking about?"

Ginger lifted her head in surprise. "I didn't know—"

"Honey, this is Justin Wainwright, Archy's son and the local sheriff. He came along to make sure you were all right."

"What did they do?" Justin asked.

Ginger bit down on her bottom lip and looked away. "N-nothing. I guess I was being silly, but they were waiting outside the door when I came out and started down the hall after me. It made me nervous and I went in there," she explained, pointing to the ladies' room. "But when I peeked out, they were always there, waiting. So I stayed inside until I heard you."

"You did the right thing, Ginger," Justin said. "Better to err on the side of caution. Have you seen them before?"

"No, I don't think they come to the club."

Joe choked back a laugh. "No, they didn't look like the country-club type."

"But you got a look at them, didn't you, Joe?"

"Yeah, a glance."

"Could either of you describe them to an artist?"

Joe pulled Ginger close to him again as he thought about what he'd seen. Regretfully, he shook his head, as did Ginger.

"Okay. But if either of you sees them anywhere, I want you to call at once. Come on, let's go back to Dad's. He'll be waiting for us."

Ginger's eyes widened in surprise but Joe didn't explain as he pulled her along with him. Outside, Justin said, "Sit in the back with Ginger. I imagine she's still a little nervous."

Joe quickly agreed. The need to feel her against him, to know she was safe, was important to him, too.

"I left my car at Archy's. Justin said he'd use the siren. You made the right decision about staying in the rest room."

"They probably didn't even know I was alarmed.

I think I overreacted. I hope I didn't cause any trouble," she said louder so Justin could hear her.

"No, ma'am, no trouble at all. I'd like to ask you a few questions about the man with a knife Joe told me about."

She turned and glared at Joe. "It was nothing."

"I had to tell Justin, honey. These men might've been connected to him," Joe explained.

"No, they weren't. I told that guy what I knew. That was all. I don't know anything else."

"What did you know then?" Justin asked, looking into the rearview mirror.

"My friend has done nothing wrong, so I don't think I have to tell you." She pressed her lips together.

"Honey—"

Justin interrupted. "I won't force you, Ginger, but if these men are connected, it could—"

"I told you they are not."

"Yes, ma'am," Justin said in a dry tone.

They rode in silence until he stopped in front of Archy's house.

"This is Mr. Wainwright's home?" Ginger asked in awe.

"Yeah. When we were kids, it was a lot of fun living here. Now I think it would be difficult. Dad won't admit it, but the house isn't the same without my mother. They're divorced, and my mother, Kate, lives in a separate cottage on the property," Justin explained to Ginger.

"She seems very nice."

"You've met her?" Joe asked in surprise.

"Why, no, but I've waited on Mrs. Wainwright before. Sometimes I work the Empire Room on the weekends."

"Come on in, and I'll introduce you to Archy."

Joe helped Ginger out. She clung to his hand. "Joe, I don't think I should. He may not want a waitress in his house."

"Don't worry," he assured her, grateful she hadn't been there earlier when he'd revealed his marriage to Archy. "By the way, how did you do on the test?"

"I think I did well," she said with a smile. "I forgot all about that when the men scared me."

"Put them out of your mind," Joe said, his arm wrapped around her.

Archy met them at the door, waving the housekeeper away. "Come in. Everything all right?" he asked as he stuck out his hand to Ginger.

She shook his hand and said, "I think I overreacted. I'm sorry I disturbed your evening."

"Think nothing of it, little lady. Come in."

Archy was hospitable to Ginger and they spent half an hour visiting before Joe suggested they leave. He pointed out that Ginger had to work in the morning.

"You're still making your wife work?" Archy asked in surprise.

Joe sent him a rueful grin. "No, my wife insists she continue working, but she's cut back her hours."

Archy turned to Ginger. "You need to be thinking about babies, not working at the club."

Ginger appeared startled, and Justin protested Archy's interference at once.

"On that note," Joe said, standing, "I'm taking my wife home. Thanks for the evening and the advice," he said, shaking Justin's and Archy's hands.

Ginger quietly bid everyone good-night and left with Joe. In the car, she said, "They were very nice. I was afraid they would embarrass you because I'm a waitress."

Crossing his fingers, Joe said, "They would never do that, Ginger. Sorry we stayed so late."

"It's all right. It's only now ten o'clock, when I usually get home from class."

"Well, no school tomorrow night. How about we go clothes shopping tomorrow? After you get off work, we can shop and eat dinner out. That would be fun, wouldn't it?"

"I don't need any clothes." She stared straight ahead at the dark road.

He shot her a quick look. "Yes, you do. People are going to ask you to go places and do things and there won't be time to go shopping. So you not only need a dress for Saturday night, but you also need more clothes for all kinds of things."

She didn't say anything.

He let it go until they got home. Once they were safely locked in their condo, he suggested a piece of the cake she'd made for dinner earlier. "I like chocolate cake."

Ginger frowned. "I'll cut you a piece, but I don't think I need one."

"Yes, you do. All that adrenaline takes a lot out of you. Besides, as your husband, I can tell you I don't think you have anything to worry about," he assured her, waggling his eyebrows to try to raise a smile.

Ginger was still worrying, but she agreed to join him at the table.

After she took her first bite of chocolate cake, she said, "My life has changed a lot since last Friday."

"Yeah, mine, too. So much has happened in such a short time. But you'll have to admit it's been interesting," he added.

They finished their cake and rinsed the dishes.

"Ready for bed?" Joe asked, sensing some tension still in Ginger.

She ducked her head. "It's silly, I know, but—but I'm a little nervous about being alone."

"Honey, you can sleep with me if you want. I'll be happy to hold you all night."

She smiled but shook her head. "I've caused you enough problems. I'm sure I'll go to sleep quickly. I'll be fine."

"Tell you what, after you get ready for bed, you can open your door before you go to sleep. I'll stay up until you're all tucked in. I'll leave my door open, too, so I can hear you if you need something."

She leaned closer and kissed his cheek. "Thank you, Joe. You are so sweet to me."

She slipped into her bedroom and closed the door. Joe wandered over to the sofa and turned on a baseball game from the West Coast. He needed something to keep him from thinking about holding Ginger in his arms in his big bed.

He wanted to hold her for many reasons, not least of which was the hunger that was growing every day. A hunger he needed to control, because he'd promised her he wouldn't take advantage of her situation.

But he also wanted to hold her safe. Ginger may think she overreacted tonight, but he didn't. If those men hadn't been waiting for her, why did they run? No, they were waiting for Ginger. But why?

They had another leisurely breakfast, which, Ginger decided, was a lovely way to start off the day. She couldn't remember any leisure time before she married Joe.

She also discovered that returning to the routine of her job was a relief, too. She was with Daisy, able to exchange thoughts and laugh together. Though the opening for the Men's Grill wasn't until Saturday evening, they were already serving meals there. Daisy was sent there, but Ginger, too young to serve the drinks in the Men's Grill, remained in the Yellow Rose Café.

Still, even without Daisy in the room, Ginger was relaxed. Because they weren't crowded today, she had time to chat with her customers and even take a break or two.

Toward the end of lunch hour, Johnny Mercado came in. Ginger had never served him before because Erica had always insisted that he sit in her section. Erica, however, wasn't working today. One of the other waitresses told Ginger that Erica had cut down on her hours also, a couple of days before Ginger did so.

Poor Harvey Small. He must be looking to hire new waitresses.

With a smile, Ginger approached Mr. Mercado's table. Though rumored to be part of the local crime syndicate, he looked to Ginger like a nice grand-fatherly type, gray-haired and quiet.

"Good afternoon, Mr. Mercado," she said. "What may I bring you to drink?"

"Iced tea, please. And I'll have a club sandwich. It won't take long, will it?"

"No, sir. I'll put the order in right away."

"Thank you."

Ginger did as she'd promised, wondering all the while if the rumor was true.

Ginger brought his iced tea and then, when it was ready, the sandwich. "Is there anything else I can bring you?"

"No, thanks."

Since he was her last customer, she went behind the partition that kept customers from seeing the kitchen and perched on a stool. If she was going to shop this afternoon, she should save her feet as much as possible.

Startled by the ring of a telephone, she peeked around the partition to see Mr. Mercado answering his cell phone. She sat back on the stool, leaning her head against the wall.

"Ricky? That you? I've been worried."

She realized she was hearing Mr. Mercado's phone conversation, but she was sure it didn't matter. Besides, she had nowhere else to sit.

"A success? You mean Luke and Westin are all right?" After a pause, he said, "Oh, no! That's terrible!"

Ginger decided half a conversation wasn't very satisfying. Besides, she didn't know who Luke and Westin were.

"No, there's not much going on around here—oh, except there was a kidnapping. That baby they found out on the golf course—she was taken from the Carson ranch."

Ginger straightened from the wall. The man was talking about Daisy's baby.

"I don't know, Ricky. Frank seems to think so. I want to believe it, but it's been a long time since they told us Haley died. If Haley is alive, why wouldn't she let us know?"

Ginger wondered who Haley was and what she was to Mr. Mercado.

"Yeah, I know Frank was crazy about her, but— You could be right. Okay, I'll keep my eye on him. When will you be back?"

He picked up a quarter of his sandwich and took a bite. "That soon? Good, we can go to the opening of the Men's Grill together Saturday night. Hurry home, son."

Well, at least now she knew who Ricky was. Did Joe know him? Should she say anything to him about it? No, she didn't think so. It was none of her business. What could it matter, anyway?

She got off the stool and took a pitcher of iced tea to the man's table to refill his drink.

She only had half an hour before she could go home. She was discovering a lot of pleasure in her new schedule, thanks to Joe.

"Hi, honey. Got time to serve me a hamburger?" Joe asked as he slid into a booth in Ginger's section.

"Of course. But there's plenty of food at home," she reminded him.

"Yeah, but we're going shopping. I don't want to take the time to go home and fix lunch. Have you eaten yet?"

"No, I don't want to eat free when I'm leaving at two."

Joe sighed but he had a grin on his face. "Lady, you are too tenderhearted. Order two hamburgers to go."

"What do you want on them?" she asked with a frown.

"Everything but onions since we're going shopping. Put what you want on the other one."

Shaking her head, she went back to the kitchen.

When they left a few minutes later, Ginger carried the sack with their lunch. Once they were in the car, they started eating.

"I hope you don't mind, but I asked my mother and Amy to come with us."

"Okay. Do they need to shop, too?"

Joe chuckled. "No. But I figured you might have questions about what would be appropriate for Saturday night, and I wouldn't have the answers. That's why Amy is coming along. Mom is there to make sure you buy enough."

She stared at him, horror on her face. "That—that's rotten! I don't want to buy a lot of clothes. That would be wasting your money!"

He was still grinning. "I want to be proud of my wife! You're beautiful, Ginger. I want everyone to know it."

"Is this part of being your wife so people will believe us?"

"Exactly." Joe knew that tactic would work. He changed the subject. "How was work today? Were you crowded?"

"No, not at all. Uh, do you know who Johnny Mercado is?"

He frowned. "Yeah, why?"

"I just wondered. The other waitresses say he's like my stepfather, but he seems very nice."

"I'm not sure what the truth is, honey, but let's not hang around him. We've got enough to deal with."

"Okay," she said agreeably.

When they got to his mother's house, Amy was already there. She'd made her husband take half a day off and come baby-sit the kids, which she thought was a good idea.

Joe pulled her aside. "Amy, I've already told Mom, but I want Ginger dressed from the skin out.

She'll protest buying anything. Try to hide the price tags and tell her it's expected for my wife to dress nicely. People will think I'm a failure if she isn't dressed well."

"Joe, surely I won't have to go that far," Amy said with a laugh.

"Yeah, you will. Especially for the underwear, because she'll point out it can't be seen. She's had a rough life. I want to make her happy. But we'll have to force her."

Several hours later, Amy understood what Joe had meant. Only following Joe's advice enabled her to convince Ginger to buy the outfits. As Joe had predicted, the underwear was especially difficult to get her to buy. Mrs. Turner helped there.

"But, dear, you want to please your husband when— I mean, every bride wants to tempt her husband."

Ginger's cheeks flamed and she hurriedly agreed, not protesting again until she caught sight of the price tag for one lacy bra in sky blue. "That's too expensive!" she exclaimed.

"Oh, no, dear, it's well worth it," Vivian said. "That's the exact color of your eyes."

"It's not her eyes he'll be looking at," Amy whispered, chuckling.

Thursday was another long day for Ginger. Joe thought about trying to convince her to skip school, but he decided that would be wrong of him. After two o'clock Friday, she would have the rest of the day and the entire weekend free.

Except for Saturday evening when she would appear at the opening as his wife and make every man there jealous. Amy and his mother had helped her select a blue watered-taffeta sheath the exact color of her eyes. When she'd come out of the dressing room to seek his approval, she'd taken his breath away.

Remembering the way she looked wasn't good for his blood pressure. Or his self-control. And he had to stay in control because he needed to stay close to her to make sure she was safe.

So here he was sitting in his car at the club, fifteen minutes early, to pick her up. Maybe he'd go in and find her. That would be better than just sitting here. The air was warming up and he didn't like getting hot.

Inside, he found a lot of people still dining in the café. He grabbed a small table and asked Ginger for a soda when she had a minute. At least here he could watch her work. Her graceful movements and friendly smile told him why she was so popular.

When two o'clock rolled around, she set a plate of nachos in front of him.

"What's this? Aren't we ready to leave?"

"Mr. Small needs me to stay another half hour and he said maybe you wouldn't mind if you had something to munch on."

He glared at her. "You're supposed to get off at two. You have a class tonight."

"Please, Joe? It's just half an hour. Or as soon as my tables clear. It won't be that long."

"I suppose so, but I don't like it."

"Pedro put extra cheese on the nachos," she told him with a smile.

He sniffed the nachos and pretended to be overcome by the aroma. "Oh, well, in that case…" Then he gave her a stern look. "Two-thirty, no longer. You need to rest."

To his surprise, she kissed him on the cheek and sang out, "Yes, dear, whatever you say." Then she danced away to the kitchen.

He grinned at the nachos. She was getting sassy now that she was getting some rest. He liked that. But he suspected she'd have him wrapped around her finger in no time—if she hadn't already.

His mother had told him last night how much she'd enjoyed herself. Amy had always been her favorite daughter-in-law, but already Ginger was a close second. Unfortunately, she'd gone on to say as soon as she gave his mother grandchildren, Ginger would be as much a favorite as Amy.

Those words brought to mind a picture of Ginger holding a redheaded baby in her arms and giving Joe that teasing smile she'd just used. He'd never thought about having children. Now, however, he would give anything to know that his future included Ginger and their children.

Ginger appeared beside him. "I'm ready now. See, it only took twenty minutes. You haven't even finished your nachos."

"I wanted to save some for you, sweetheart." He shoved the platter toward her. She slipped into the seat across from him and ate a couple. His hunger had returned and he joined her. In no time, the platter was empty.

"I'll take this to the kitchen and wipe off the table. Then we can go," she assured him with a grin.

He rose and moved to the hall that led to the parking lot.

Quickly she joined him and slipped her arm in his. "I'm going to wear my new jeans and the dark blue sweater when I get home. Thank you so much for my beautiful new clothes."

"My pleasure, honey. Since I get to see you in them, it really is my pleasure." He leaned over and kissed her soft lips.

She made no objection at first. Her lips were soft and sweet and he couldn't help himself. But then she jerked away. "We mustn't do that. There's no one watching." She pulled her hand away and rushed down the hall in front of him.

Joe didn't try to catch up. Maybe they both needed a little distance.

But when he came through the door and saw the same two men from Tuesday night dragging Ginger toward a nearby car, he changed his mind.

Eight

"Stop!" Joe shouted, charging the two men. Movement out of the corner of his eye showed him one of the kitchen workers having a cigarette, staring openmouthed at the situation. "Go call 911! Hurry!"

Ginger appeared to bite one of the men who was trying to hold a handkerchief to her nose. She wobbled a little, but Joe grabbed the other man's arm and jerked him away from Ginger. As he did so, he ordered, "Scream, Ginger, as loud as you can."

She emitted an earsplitting scream even as she kneed the man yelling at her in protest. The man Joe had hold of managed to send a blow to his jaw, but it glanced off as Joe pulled back. Then Joe got in a belly blow that took the man's breath away. Using his advantage, Joe hit him in the nose. Then he turned to help Ginger.

She, however, had slammed both fists together to the top of the man's head as he'd bent over from her knee attack and he was down on the ground. Ginger ran to Joe, back in his arms again.

"Joe, are you all right?"

"I'm fine. Go inside and find some rope."

"I don't want to leave you alone!" she exclaimed.

"Don't worry—"

The door opened and several of the men who bussed tables poured out into the parking lot, quickly followed by Harvey Small.

"What's going on out here?" the manager asked.

"These two men were trying to kidnap Ginger. Did you call the police?" Joe asked the man he'd seen earlier.

The man shook his head and looked at Harvey.

"Harvey, tell him to call 911. These men are going to jail." Joe was ready to throw a few more punches if someone didn't call the police. Harvey looked at him and then nodded to his employee.

After the man hurried back inside, Joe looked at the club manager. "Good decision, Harvey, or you were going to be next."

"Why would anyone try to kidnap Ginger? She's worked here over a year now without anyone bothering her. This is ridiculous."

"That's not true. But it doesn't matter. They tried today. If you ask the guy who went to call the police, he'll tell you."

About that time, the man Joe had fought tried to get up.

"Stay down, or I'm going to hit you again," Joe warned.

The man ignored him and tried to run for the car. Joe suddenly realized the doors were open and the motor was running. He took a flying leap and landed on the man's back, knocking him to the ground. "Ginger, get the car keys!" he ordered. He didn't think any of the employees were going to help unless

Harvey gave the order, and he didn't have time to wait.

He controlled the man and shouted again for rope. He was afraid the other man would escape because he was recovering a few feet away. The distant sound of sirens encouraged him, however.

Ginger appeared in his view, a heavy skillet in her hand, as she moved to stand over the second man. "If you move, I'll crack your skull. Stay down on the ground."

Joe almost laughed at Ginger's fierce tone. She always sounded so sweet. He sat on his victim and looked at his gentle wife. "Good job, Ginger."

"Will Justin be the one who comes?"

"If he's not, we'll call him. These are the two guys from Tuesday night."

"Yes, I recognize them."

A sheriff's car screeched to a halt and two men jumped out, one of them drawing his gun. "What's going on?"

Joe got off the man on the pavement and pulled him to his feet. "These two men tried to kidnap my wife."

"Kidnap? Are you sure?" the deputy asked as he took handcuffs and slapped them on the man.

Joe picked up the handkerchief the other man had tried to hold to Ginger's nose. He gave it to the deputy. "They tried to hold this over her nose. Smell it."

"Ether. I guess you're right."

"Yeah. Call Justin Wainwright, please. He asked

us to call him if we saw these characters again. This is the second attempt.''

The other deputy, having cuffed the other man and put him in the back seat of the car, used his radio to request Justin's attention.

Harvey reluctantly invited them to come in for coffee while they waited, but they refused, saying Justin would be there in five minutes.

In the meantime, they wanted to get as much information as possible from Joe and Ginger.

Ginger seemed reluctant to say anything, and Joe had to admit he wasn't sure why they were after Ginger. He was relieved when he heard the siren that signaled Justin's arrival.

After Joe and Ginger confirmed that these were the two men from Tuesday night, Justin sent the deputies back to headquarters with the order to file kidnapping charges against the two men and start questioning them.

Then Justin turned back to Joe. ''I think this could be connected to the mob in New York. They obviously had no intention to hurt her…right now. But it's possible there will be other attempts. Why don't you two go stay at Dad's for a few days?''

Ginger gasped and turned pleading eyes to Joe.

He looked at her and then back at Justin. ''You think that's necessary?''

''I don't think you should make it easy for them. Ginger needs to have someone with her at all times. And why stay where they know you live?''

''You've got a point. Okay, but we'll go to Mom

and Dad's. It would be too much of an imposition to go to Archy's.''

"You know Dad wouldn't think so. You might keep it in mind for later.'' Justin added, "Go pack your things now and get out of there before these guys get cut free by some lawyer.''

"You think they will?'' Joe asked in outrage.

"They always do, Joe. Money's no object when it comes to lawyers for the mob. We're going to find out all we can before that happens. I'll let you know how it goes.''

"Right. Thanks, Justin.''

After Justin had driven off, Joe took Ginger's hand. But instead of heading to the car, he led her back into the club to Harvey's office.

"Harvey, Ginger won't be working here anymore. It makes it too easy for someone to find her,'' he said.

"You can't do that to me! I don't have enough waitresses as it is!'' Harvey protested.

With sarcasm, Joe said, "I think Ginger's safety is more important than people having to wait a little longer for their food. It doesn't matter. We're not offering you a choice. We're telling you how it's going to be.''

"I'm sorry, Mr. Small,'' Ginger said softly.

Joe was glad she didn't argue with him. She seemed to realize how serious her situation was.

He wrapped his arm around her shoulders and led her back out to the car. Once they started to the condo, he said, "When we get back home, gather up all your new clothes and anything else you want with you. We're going to use your car and leave mine parked there as a decoy.''

''Joe, will I be able to go to school?''

He regretted what he had to say. He'd hoped to improve her life, but that didn't seem to be happening. ''Honey, I'm sorry, but I don't see how you can. Until we figure out what's going on, you can't go to school. If things wind up fast, your teachers will take you back. But I can't promise anything.''

She quietly nodded. No tears, no pleading, just acceptance. He squeezed her hand in support and admiration.

Once inside, he did a quick packing job for himself. Then he called his maid Maria's number and left word that they were going out of town for a while. He said he would drop a check in the mail for the month, but she didn't need to come to work. He'd contact her later.

When he checked on Ginger, he found she was trying to pack everything into her two small bags.

''Just leave them in the boxes. I'll stick them in the trunk like that. We'll get some luggage as soon as we can so you can properly pack.''

As she gathered everything up, he went back to the phone. ''Mom? Ginger and I need to come over for a few days. I'll explain to you and Dad when we get there. And Mom, you can't tell anyone, even my brothers, that we're there. Okay?''

''Okay,'' his mother said, quiet acceptance in her

voice, just like Ginger, though he knew she must be curious.

"Thanks, Mom. We'll be there in about fifteen minutes. I'm going to park in the back."

"Better the garage, son. Sounds like we need to keep it secret."

"You're right, Mom. Thanks. We'll see you in a few minutes."

When he looked for Ginger, he found her in the kitchen. She was packing up some of the groceries they'd bought. "We don't want the groceries to go to waste. Your mother can store and use them while we're there."

Joe started to tell her to throw them out, but Ginger was right. Besides, the two men couldn't have gotten out of jail this quickly. "I'll start loading the car," he said.

Fifteen minutes later, they got in the Honda and drove to Joe's childhood home. He pulled into the drive and drove straight through to the garage, which already had the door open.

"Go inside through the back door, honey," Joe instructed Ginger. "I'll start bringing things in."

She nodded, as if in accord, but went on her way regardless. She gathered two heavy sacks of groceries and carried them to the door.

Joe smiled and nodded. "You're a good partner, Ginger Turner."

Ginger knocked on the back door and it quickly opened. Mrs. Turner held the door open for her and then reached for one of the grocery bags. "You brought food?"

"I didn't want it to ruin." She also didn't want to do the explaining. It seemed a terrible imposition, but Joe seemed to think it would be all right.

She followed the woman to the kitchen and set down her sack. "I'm going to go help Joe bring in our clothes." She hurried out the back again, only to meet Joe coming in loaded down. "Is there anything else?"

"Yeah, some boxes and your smaller bag."

"I'll get them. Shall I close the garage door before I come in?"

Mrs. Turner said, "I'll go with you and close up. That garage door opener is tricky. We really need to get a new one."

When they were all safely back in the house, with their car hidden in the garage, Joe's mother invited them to the kitchen so they could have some coffee and Joe could tell her what was wrong.

"Now," she said, filling Joe's mug, "what's happened? Are you moving in for a while? You know you're welcome anytime."

"Thanks, Mom. Um, some men tried to kidnap Ginger today." She looked alarmed and he felt a shiver run through Ginger, who was sitting very close to him, holding his hand.

"What? Why? What's going on?"

The conversation was halted because Ed Turner came in the back door. "Well, hi, son, Ginger. didn't know you were coming to visit."

Vivian Turner repeated Joe's statement to her husband. His reaction was much as hers had been—questions.

Joe held up his hand. "I'm glad you came in, Dad, so I'll only have to explain once." He told them about the attempt Tuesday night, about Ginger calling her mother. Then the call he'd received, and Justin's recommendation. "He suggested we go to Archy's, but I'd rather stay here if y'all don't mind. I think Ginger will be more comfortable here."

"But, Joe," Ginger protested, "it might put them in danger. I hadn't thought of that until now. Maybe I should just...go away." She paused, as if thinking about her options. "Yes, I think that's what I should do. I can move to another town and—and hide. They won't find me."

The Turners stared at her. Then Vivian said, "But Joe is your husband, and we are your family. Of course you can't go. You two need to be together."

Ed nodded. "That's right."

Tears filled Ginger's eyes. "You don't have to—"

"Yes, they do, sweetheart. You're not going away. You're my wife and I'm going to protect you."

"With our help," Vivian added.

Joe suggested Ginger go lie down and rest. Her face was still paler than normal.

His mother took Ginger's arm and led her to the stairs. "I've put you in Joe's old bedroom. But it's not a museum. I've updated it and it's become our best guest room."

"I'm sure it will be fine, Mrs. Turner. It's so nice of you to offer to help."

Vivian stared at her. "Nice? It's what families do. And call me Vivian, child. That's what all my daughters-in-law call me. That way I don't feel so old," she added with a teasing grin. Before Ginger could respond, Vivian added, "And now is when you tell me I'm not old. I love that part."

Ginger smiled, relaxing for the first time since the incident at the club. "Of course you're not old."

"Nicely done, child. Now, put your feet up and rest. I'm making a special dinner. We're celebrating tonight."

"What are we celebrating?" Ginger asked, confused.

"That we're all safe and together. That's a lot to be grateful for." Vivian leaned over and kissed Ginger's cheek before opening the nearest door. Then she turned and went back down the stairs.

Ginger stared after her. Vivian had an elevated vision of family. Her mother was one of the reasons Ginger was having difficulties now. It hurt to admit it, but her mother had caused the two men to attack her. She'd called back and found out the town she lived in. All because Ginger had been concerned about the beatings her mother said she had received. Now Ginger wondered if her mother had lied about the beatings, too.

Whatever her mother had done in the past, Ginger had never believed her mother would betray her in such a way.

But she had.

Vivian Turner was a different kind of mother. The kind of mother little girls dreamed about. Not the kind Ginger had experienced. Her mother had frequently worked as a prostitute, always to keep a roof over their heads, her mother had told her. And Ginger had believed her. Now she wasn't so sure. It had taken a lot of money to buy an American husband.

Ginger had worked from the time she was eleven, mopping the floors in a grocery store in the evening until midnight. Her mother had begun charging groceries there, the cost of which the owner deducted from Ginger's salary. Though her mother had wanted her to quit school and work full-time, Ginger had refused. The only reason she was able to stay in school was that her mother slept until noon.

When her mother had made the decision to come to America, Ginger held her breath wondering if she would accompany her mother. When her mother had agreed that Ginger should come, Ginger had dreamed of a different life.

Her life had been different, but not what she'd expected.

Her mother had discovered education was required until her daughter turned seventeen. Ginger had loved the school and the classes. Knowing she might not get to stay her senior year, she'd worked hard to get as much out of school as she could. Some of the kids made fun of her clothes and her accent, but she ignored them. She found a part-time job after school without telling her mother, who seldom cared where

Ginger was. Ginger spent a little of her money on clothes—she learned about garage sales and bought secondhand—and saved the rest. The shop owner paid her in cash, which she carefully hid in her room.

She got to stay in school her senior year and actually graduate, though there was no senior ring or dress for the prom. She treated herself to a good haircut—a short pageboy that was her big expenditure.

But immediately after school ended, her mother had suggested she marry Leo, her stepfather's boss. The old man undressed her with his eyes every time he came into the house.

Ginger had gathered up her savings and struck out on her own, with no help from family. But then, her family was nothing like Joe's loving parents who had opened their home and hearts to her.

Ginger entered Joe's old bedroom, now the ''best'' guest room. It was lovely, with three windows looking out on the backyard, covered by sheer curtains that floated a little from a breeze. The king-size bed was piled with pillows and covered by a beautiful homemade quilt that Ginger stroked with pleasure. Such exquisite artistry. She pulled back the quilt, not wanting to harm it in any way, and lay down on the violet sheets under it. How could she not be happy in such a lovely room? How could she not feel safe in such a warm, inviting home? How could she ever be unhappy surrounded by that new concept—a family who helped you?

With a sigh, she closed her eyes.

* * *

Joe and his dad chatted calmly about things his brothers were doing, knowing if they discussed Joe and Ginger's situation, they'd only have to repeat it for his mom. When she came back into the kitchen, Joe cleared his throat. "I really appreciate your support, Mom, Dad."

Ed looked surprised. "Well, of course we're helping you."

"Some families don't behave that way. Like Ginger's mother."

"What do you mean?" Vivian asked in surprise. "I'm sure her mother would do her best for Ginger if she were here."

"No, Mom. I think her mother betrayed Ginger." He told them about the phone call from a woman with an accent, determining where they lived. "I'm pretty sure that was Ginger's mom."

Vivian stared at them, then covered her face with her hands. "Oh, no! How could her mother do that?"

"Ginger seems to expect very little from her mother. The strange thing about Ginger is how much she seems to be willing to do for others."

"She's a sweet girl," Ed said. "A good addition to the family, boy."

Guilt filled Joe. He already knew it was going to kill him when Ginger left him. He'd made a miscalculation when he'd thought he could pretend to be her husband to help her and then walk away with no damage. But he didn't want to hurt his family. "Don't get too attached to her."

"What do you mean?" Vivian asked in alarm.

"Do you think they'll succeed in taking her away? We'll get Justin to protect her."

"I'll protect her!" Joe protested, not wanting to put that responsibility on anyone else. After all, he was her husband...for now.

"I need to tell you something, but you won't be able to tell anyone, even if it means lying." Joe watched his parents' faces. He knew how much they'd emphasized honesty as he was growing up.

Ed looked him straight in the eye. "Go ahead and tell us."

"I married Ginger to help her. She's— The INS was going to take her away. I didn't think it was fair. I've always admired Ginger and I offered to marry her to help her get her green card."

Vivian gasped. "Oh, dear!"

He hurriedly added, "She's beautiful, of course, but she has such a genuine goodness about her. She's so hardworking. She was working seventy hours a week. She rode the bus or walked everywhere. Her apartment was one room and she slept on the couch. Helping her seemed such an easy thing to do."

Vivian, after staring at him, relaxed with a smile. "But it's not easy now, is it?" she asked softly, leaning forward.

"Well, no. I didn't realize she would be in such trouble."

"That's not what I mean, and you know it. You love her, don't you?"

Joe shrugged his shoulders, trying to avoid such a confession. "She's a good person."

"Yes, she is," Ed agreed, staring at his wife, as if he didn't quite comprehend what his wife was getting at.

Vivian just kept smiling at her son. Joe tried to look away, but his mother had always been good about eliciting a confession. Finally, he said, "Okay, I love her. But that doesn't change our agreement. I'm an old man to Ginger. She appreciates my help and does anything she thinks I want her to do. But she doesn't think of me as her husband. Not really."

"You mean the two of you haven't—" Ed shifted his eyes to look at his wife, then turned back to Joe. "You haven't, uh, made love?"

"No. And when the INS asks you if our marriage is real, you'll have to lie."

"No, we won't, Joe," Vivian said firmly.

"Yes, you will."

"No. I've seen the marriage certificate. I know you love her. And I don't ask what happens behind closed doors. I'll just say you'd better be married or I would never let you share a room in my house."

"But, Mom, we're not sharing a room."

"Oh, yes, you are," Vivian assured him with a twinkle in her eyes.

Nine

Joe climbed the stairs slowly, not that he wasn't anxious to see Ginger. He could admit to himself that he missed her, worried about her. But he couldn't admit that to Ginger. He was her friend, nothing more.

The friend who was going to wake her up for dinner, now that she'd slept the afternoon away.

He opened the door slowly. "Ginger?" he called from the doorway. "Ginger, Mom's making dinner. Ready to come down?"

No movement. He called a little louder. "Ginger!" He crossed the room until he stood by the wide, comfortable bed. He reached out and gently touched her arm. "Ginger?"

She opened her big blue eyes and smiled at him.

"Hi, Joe. Is something wrong?"

"No, sweetheart. Mom is fixing dinner and thought you might want to have a few minutes to pull yourself together. Dinner is almost ready."

"Oh, I should've offered to help," she said, sliding out of the bed. She was fully clothed and Joe smiled ruefully. He shouldn't have been thinking about the possibility of her being in her underwear. But he had.

As soon as she was standing up, she carefully made the bed so it looked as good as it had when she entered.

Would she leave his life the same way, with no sign of her having been part of it? No, he knew that wouldn't happen. He would never forget Ginger. Her innocence, her goodness, her beauty. "Ginger," he began, intending to tell her they would have to share the room.

Ginger interrupted, "I think it would be rude to eat dinner without helping. We can talk later on." She hurried out the door and down the stairs.

Joe stood there, in the silence of the room he'd grown up in. Things had changed a lot in twenty-five years, since he was nine and sure the world would be a wonderful place. Now he wanted to make it a wonderful place for *Ginger,* with or without him.

He slid his hands into his pockets. Ginger hadn't had the advantages he'd received—wonderful parents, four loving brothers, a quality education, a good job—but it hadn't stopped Ginger from trying. He'd find a way to help her. He'd keep her here in America. Somehow.

By the end of dinner Vivian's warmth had made Ginger feel at home. It hadn't taken long to do the dishes, with all the conveniences. And the friendship Vivian extended made it an enjoyable experience.

"Let's take a coffee tray into the living room," Vivian suggested. "Ed likes his coffee while he watches his favorite shows."

"I don't even know if Joe has favorite shows," Ginger remarked. "Does he?"

"I don't know, dear. He hasn't lived at home in years. We'll ask him."

Once they were in the room, Vivian interrupted Ed. "Joe, Ginger wants to know if you have favorite shows you like to watch."

Both Joe and his father frowned. Then Joe said, "What difference does it make?"

"I just wondered," Ginger said. "Your mother knows what shows your father likes."

Joe grinned. "Don't worry about it, sweetheart. I'm not that committed to any television show."

"What do you do with yourself?" Ginger asked.

"Tonight, I've been talking about building my dream house. Now that I've decided to live here, it's time to start it."

"Do you have pictures of it?"

"I have plans. Want to see them?"

Ginger was thrilled to be included in Joe's future. It wouldn't last, but for a little while at least, she was part of Joe's future. Part of a family.

A couple of hours later, Ed and Vivian said goodnight. Joe stood and held out his hand to Ginger. "Ready to go to bed? It's been a pretty active day."

"Yes, it's not often you get kidnapped," Ginger said with a weary smile. "But I love your house, Joe."

"I like the changes you suggested. You and Mom were great."

"Your mother, mostly. She's very good. And her cooking is wonderful."

"She does a lot in the community, too. But I'm afraid you can't go out with her. I want you to stay hidden."

She frowned. "Won't that mean you have to stay hidden, too?"

"Well, for a few days."

"I don't like this. It's not fair to you."

He stared at her. "Ginger, my job is to keep you safe. Don't forget that. Even after you get your green card, when you'll have the right to do what you want, I'll still keep an eye on you."

"Joe, you are so good to me." She leaned over and kissed his cheek. Then she turned and hurried up the stairs.

Joe stood at the bottom of the stairs until he remembered that he was going to the same bedroom. And he hadn't told Ginger yet.

He hurried up the stairs.

The bedroom door was already closed. He tapped lightly and called, "Ginger."

She opened the door immediately. "Yes, Joe?"

"Uh, Ginger, this is my bedroom, too. Mom thinks we share a bed since we're married, and we can't tell her otherwise."

He watched as Ginger stared at him, shock in her eyes. "Ginger, I don't mean we have to— I mean, of course I won't expect you to— I can sleep on the floor."

Ginger looked at him, then at the bed and the floor. "The floor is hard."

"Yeah, but I'll manage. I'll take a pillow and a blanket and—"

"No, of course not. It's a big bed. We can share without— We can manage."

"You're sure? It will be more comfortable for me, but—"

"You are sacrificing enough for me, Joe. It's the least I can do."

Joe moved into the room cautiously, as if he thought she'd change her mind. "Do you intend to take a bath tonight?"

"I'd like to, if it's not too much trouble."

"No, that'll be fine. I'll unpack while you bathe."

She quickly took some things out of her suitcase and hurried into the bathroom, as if she felt safe in there. Joe unpacked his own clothes, using the chest of drawers. Then he unpacked Ginger's clothes also, trying to avoid lingering over the silky things his mother had insisted she buy. Imagining Ginger in those items created too much tension.

When Ginger came out, wrapped in his own terry-cloth robe, he resisted looking at her. "I put your things in that dresser. You can put your dirty clothes in the hamper in the bathroom. Mom will get them."

"I will do our laundry."

"Okay, you can get them in the morning. Or maybe I will. I can do laundry, too, you know."

She nodded. "You can have the bathroom now."

"Thanks. Uh, what side of the bed do you want?"

She hesitated. "If you don't mind, I would like the side by the window. I like to see the stars at night."

"Okay." He crossed to the drawers where he'd put his belongings, suddenly realizing he didn't have any pajamas. Normally he slept in his underwear. What was he going to do now?

A knock on the door stopped him. He opened the door and discovered his mother waiting. "Yes, Mom?"

"Do you need to borrow your father's pajama bottoms, dear?"

Joe breathed a sigh of relief. "Thanks, Mom. I'll be right there."

He closed the door and faced Ginger. "Um, I won't be long, but go ahead and go to sleep if you're tired." *Please go to sleep.* He didn't want to deal with the temptation of whatever she wore under the robe. If his mother picked it out, he didn't think he'd be able to resist. She was a wicked woman when it came time to tempt a man.

When he returned ten minutes later, he saw Ginger on the side of the bed by the window. She was clutching the edge of the mattress as if she feared she would fall off. Her eyes were tightly shut.

"Ginger, are you all right?"

She nodded her head, not speaking.

"Ginger, I can sleep on the floor if it will make you feel better."

"No, there's a lot of room."

She was right, but he was definitely attracted to

the area she was occupying. He could see baby-blue straps on her shoulders and could only imagine what was beneath the sheet. Slowly, he lifted the sheet and slid under the covers.

If anything, he felt more tension when he couldn't see her. Because he could feel her warm body even though it was at least three feet away. He'd never realized how big a king-size bed was until tonight.

"Ginger, if you don't relax, you'll never go to sleep." He waited until she slowly did so. "It's going to be all right, Ginger, I promise."

"I just didn't want to cause you any trouble, Joe. Thank you for taking care of me."

"My pleasure," he whispered.

Ginger woke up just as the sun was coming over the rooftops, shining directly into the windows of Joe's bedroom. It was almost April, and in south Texas, that was warm, bright air, bathing the world in gold. She lay there, thinking about the twists and turns in her life. She couldn't imagine being more comfortable, more relaxed anywhere in the world. Joe's arm tightened around her— Joe's arm?

She froze, not daring to take a breath. Joe had his arm around her. It felt nice, safe. But, of course, he must have moved in his sleep. He couldn't realize what he was doing. He'd be embarrassed if he awoke now. She inched away from him, sliding out of the bed.

She watched him shift under the covers, but he settled down quickly. Holding her breath, she tiptoed away from the bed, grabbing her robe on her way. Well, Joe's robe, actually, but the only one she had. She slipped into it and tied the belt. Then she crossed to the drawers where he'd put her clothes. When she'd found a pair of jeans and a blouse, she carried them into the bathroom. All the time she changed and brushed her hair, she thought of Joe, lying in bed, sleeping peacefully. She wished she were there with him. She wished she could wake up with his arms around her, and simply turn over and cuddle with him.

She knew enough about men to know Joe probably wouldn't complain about sex. But he would complain about being caught and tied to a woman. Joe didn't want that. Otherwise he would have married long ago, like his brothers. She couldn't do that to him.

She entered the bedroom to find Joe still sleeping. She moved away from the bed, so she wouldn't be tempted. Instead, she hurried to the door and opened it, slipping outside and closing the door. She headed for the kitchen.

Putting on a pot of coffee, she began organizing breakfast. It was only six-thirty, but she figured Ed and Vivian would be up soon. Sure enough, half an hour later, she heard sounds upstairs. By that time, she had cinnamon rolls in the oven. When Ed and Vivian came down the stairs, the aroma of homemade cinnamon rolls pervaded the air.

"My, something smells good," Vivian said.

Ed was on her heels, his nose up, breathing deeply.

"Smells like the doughnut shop on the square," Ed added.

"I made cinnamon rolls. I thought you might like them."

"We'll love them, Ginger," Vivian said with a smile. "I had no idea you could make these."

"I learned when I was a little girl."

"Boy, Joe shouldn't have kept these a secret," Ed said, taking a seat at the table while his wife poured him a cup of coffee.

"It's not often I find coffee already made," Vivian added.

"You deserve a break. I'll cook some bacon, too."

The three of them were enjoying a leisurely breakfast when Joe came down.

His mother and father greeted him casually, and Ginger tried to do the same.

He stepped to her side and kissed her cheek. "Good morning. I didn't mean to sleep so late."

"You didn't. I woke up early. I thought I'd make cinnamon rolls for breakfast," Ginger said.

"You made the cinnamon rolls? You didn't go buy them?"

"Of course, you told me not to go out."

He smiled at her. "I should've known better." Then he looked at his father. "Well, are they any good?"

Ed grinned. "They're terrible, absolutely terrible. Better give them to me. I'll get rid of them."

Ginger looked upset and Joe put his arm around

her. "Dad's teasing, trying to keep all of them to himself."

"Are you sure you like them, Ed? You don't have to eat any—" Ginger began, hurt on her face.

"Oh, honey, I love 'em," Ed assured her. "I was teasing Joe."

Since Joe took that moment to bite into a roll, everyone stared at him. He closed his eyes as he savored the sweet taste. "Mercy, Ginger, you made these? They're fabulous. I bet you could start a bakery and be rich in no time!"

Ginger was consoled. "Thank you, Joe. But they're just cinnamon rolls."

"Have you already eaten?"

"Yes, I ate with your parents. But I'll be glad to keep you company." She sat back down beside him and poured him coffee. Then she poured herself a little more.

"Heck, I'm in no hurry," Ed exclaimed, and reached for another cinnamon roll. Vivian, however, stopped him.

"You've had three already and you're supposed to be in early this morning. Come along. I've laid out your clothes." Grabbing him by the arm, she hauled her husband up the stairs.

Joe frowned as he stared after them. Then he turned back to Ginger. "I think Mom is trying to give us some time alone together."

Ginger seemed flustered. "I'm sure she isn't. She probably wants me to do the dishes."

"How are you this morning?" he asked abruptly.

"I'm fine, of course. That's a very comfortable bed."

Joe watched her as she began gathering up his parents' dishes. "Sit down and talk to me while I eat." When she settled herself comfortably, he asked, "I didn't disturb you last night, did I?"

"No, of course not. I didn't wake up at all until the sun came up this morning."

"We'll have to start closing the shades before we go to bed at night."

"I like getting up with the sun. I can get more done that way, like the laundry."

Joe grinned. "Laundry won't take that long, Ginger. You've got all day." He couldn't imagine what she would do for the rest of the day. "I'll be working on some plans for a government project the mayor's supposedly opening up. Maybe there's something you can help Mom with."

"Maybe I can do all the cooking."

"I don't think Mom will give that up. But we'll see what we can find for you to do."

Vivian came into the kitchen at that moment. "Sorry to interrupt, but Ed needs another cup of coffee."

"Please, Vivian, is there something for me to do? I'll do the dishes, but after that, I don't know—"

"Oh, I'm so glad you asked. I'm making some baby blankets for Kitty—Rodney's wife, you know. I could certainly use some help."

"Oh, I would love to help you. I've sewn quite a bit."

Joe gave his mother a thumbs-up. He was pleased that Ginger would have something to occupy her time while he worked on his ideas for houses.

"Finish your breakfast and go away, Joe," Vivian said, tongue-in-cheek. "Ginger and I have things to do."

As easy as that, Ginger was taken care of. Suddenly, she had no time for Joe. And she seemed happy about it. As he went away, he tried to hide his disgruntled attitude.

Justin called that night.

"I'm thinking Ginger didn't go to class tonight, right? I had some men watching, but no one showed up."

"Do you think we're overreacting?" Joe didn't think so, since they'd already tried twice to get her.

"No. Just as I suspected, those two goons got out. Kept their mouths shut while they were here. It may take a little time for them to set something else up, but I suspect they'll keep trying."

"Me, too. I'm keeping her hidden here for now. If necessary, I can take her away somewhere for a belated honeymoon or something."

Justin chuckled. "No rest for the weary, huh?"

"Right." Justin had no idea how hard that would be for Joe, since he couldn't touch her. He had last night, however. He'd held her in his arms all night long. Now he shrugged away even the thought of a belated honeymoon. "I won't do that unless it's necessary."

"Well, keep your eyes open. You never know who will turn up."

"Will do. Thanks for helping out, Justin."

"No problem. Call me if you get suspicious."

After Joe hung up the phone, he stared into space. Ginger had already gone upstairs for her bath. Joe had planned on staying downstairs until after Ginger was in bed, hopefully asleep, before he entered the room. That would be safer. He wondered if he could hold Ginger in her sleep again, and if she'd been aware of it. If she had, she'd evidently not been bothered by it. Or she was pretending it hadn't happened.

Half an hour later, he dragged up the stairs and pushed open the door to their bedroom. The room was dark, but he could see Ginger's body outlined against the light through the window.

He gathered his belongings and hurriedly tiptoed into the bathroom. After a shower—cold, in case he needed it—he dried off and put on clean underwear and pajamas and T-shirt. Then he tiptoed across the room again and slid into the bed.

Ginger had seemed happy today. She'd sewed with his mother all morning, doing exquisite work, according to Vivian. The two women had fixed lunch together for the three of them. Then Vivian had given Ginger a book to read. When he'd asked what it was, he discovered it was some mystery his mother had enjoyed. She said Ginger shouldn't have to work all day.

Ginger had begun reading and Joe had heard little out of her the rest of the day. After eating supper and cleaning up, Ginger had returned to her book until she finished it about an hour ago. She told Vivian it was a wonderful book. Then, telling them all good-night, she'd gone upstairs.

"A delightful girl," Vivian said.

"Yes, she is."

"Yes, but I mean delightful because she's a hard worker, and very pleasant to be with," Vivian said. "I don't mean because she's beautiful."

"But she is beautiful," Joe protested.

"I know," Vivian said.

Joe thought about those words as he climbed the stairs. His mother was right. Even if she weren't beautiful, Ginger was a great person. And fortunate, to have both beauty and goodness.

He stared at her again, wrapped in the covers, her back turned to him.

He got into bed, careful not to awaken her. After a moment of holding very still, he relaxed, feeling sure she was already asleep.

"Joe?"

He jumped sky-high. "Ginger! I thought you were asleep."

"No. I need to ask you something."

"Well, sure, honey. Ask away."

Without turning toward him, she simply said, "What's so special about being a virgin?"

Ten

Ginger had considered asking Vivian, but couldn't face her. She thought she could in the dark, with Joe. He was such a thoughtful, gentle man.

"Why do you ask?" He spoke in a level, calm voice. She sat up in bed, shoving down the cover, forgetting she had on a low-cut nightgown.

"When I was with my mother and she tried to talk me into marrying Leo, she said—"

Joe sat up, too, stuffing a pillow behind him. "What did she say?"

"That he'd only want me a few times, until I definitely wasn't a virgin anymore, then I could do what I wanted." She said the words fast, her face red, looking away from Joe. She couldn't look at him.

"What do you want me to explain?"

"What did she mean? Why did she say that?"

Joe groaned. "Well, Ginger, there are men who want to make love to inexperienced girls exclusively. They're slightly sick. The act of love has no meaning for them. It's a physical act that gets them excited, but they have no feelings for the woman."

She turned to stare at him. "That's disgusting."

"Yeah."

"Is it different for other men?"

"Yeah. Most men have feelings for one woman, and the two of them form a family. The sex is part of the relationship but not all of it, by any means. You could offer my father Marilyn Monroe and he'd pass her up for my mom."

"Marilyn Monroe is dead," Ginger pointed out, proud that she'd known about the American actress and sex symbol.

"Yeah, well, I meant when she was alive."

"I like that explanation. Are you that kind of man?"

"Oh, yeah."

"But you haven't married."

"No." He didn't say anything else.

"So, if I had sex with someone, would that make Leo not want me anymore?" She held her breath for the answer.

Joe turned on his side toward her. "I don't know, Ginger. It wouldn't make a normal man not want you," he said carefully.

Ginger lay there in the moonlight, thinking. She knew she was attracted to Joe. She liked being with him. She felt safe and cared for. "Joe, would you make love to me? Then our problems would be solved."

Joe went off into a coughing fit and Ginger waited helplessly for him to recover. "Are you all right?"

"Uh, yeah, I'm all right."

"Did you hear my question?"

"Yeah. I heard. Ginger, I'd love to, uh, accommodate you. It would be a great pleasure, but—but your first time to make love should be special. You should make love because you can't help yourself, because you want to spend the rest of your life with the man, no other reason.''

Ginger looked at him in surprise. ''But it will help with the green card, too, won't it? Won't they ask us about it?''

''Yeah.''

Silence reigned. Finally he shifted flat on his back again. ''But I don't think this is the time or place to, uh, advance our relationship.''

''But would you do it to protect me? Would you be willing to do that?''

''Of course I would, but it isn't going to come to that. I'll protect you without making love to you. That was our deal.''

''Thank you, Joe,'' she said in a small voice, and slid back down under the covers. She hadn't realized how much Joe had given her when he'd blithely offered to marry her for a green card. But he seemed to have.

Joe closed his eyes, praying that the conversation was over and Ginger would fade into sleep. How long he'd be awake, he didn't know.

Turning down Ginger as she lay in the bed with him, her warm curves young and fresh, her body firm yet soft, her mind free of other men, was difficult. He was sweating under the covers. Not perspiring, a dignified emission, but sweating, fighting tooth and nail the urges that told him to pull her close, to take what she offered in the guise of protection.

The temptation to claim her as his when he could, devil take the future, was so tempting. Maybe he could bind her to him, make her pregnant, tell her she owed him for his sacrifice. But he couldn't do that to sweet Ginger. She hadn't asked him to marry her, to sacrifice for her. He'd volunteered, because he thought it would be a simple thing.

But he wouldn't change what had happened. Ginger deserved her green card. She deserved to make her own choices and be safe. He'd do it again if he had to.

"Joe?"

He froze. Not more discussion, please, he silently begged.

"Yeah, Ginger?"

"You're not mad at me, are you?"

"No, Ginger, I've never been mad at you."

"Is it bad that I'm a virgin?"

"No, honey. Someday that will be a precious gift to your husband."

"You're very good to me, Joe," Ginger whispered, then said nothing else.

Joe gradually relaxed.

They spent Friday much as they had Thursday. Ginger helped sew the baby blankets and then read the afternoon away. Joe worked on house plans, occasionally interrupting his mother and Ginger for their opinions. He was surprised at how content he was, doing work he loved close to Ginger. He wasn't restless, but he worried about Ginger.

"Ginger, are you okay?" he asked about three o'clock that afternoon.

She was in the window seat in the den, propped on pillows and reading. "Yes, of course I am."

"You don't feel the need to go somewhere or do something?"

Ginger smiled. "I've never had time to sit and read in the middle of the day before. I suppose it might get boring after a while, but I'm enjoying myself. Do you need to go somewhere?"

He smiled back. "Nope. I've got my work and you. What else do I need?"

Ginger returned his smile but looked at her watch. "Oh! I'm going to fix a cassoulet for dinner tonight. I need to go get it started." She marked her place in the book and then abandoned it on the window seat. "It's a good thing you interrupted me. I'd almost forgotten."

"A cassoulet? What's that?"

"It's a type of stew we used to make a lot. We made it because we could use stew bones or small amounts of meat, but here, there's plenty of meat. It makes a very good dish." She hurried off to the kitchen, a smile on her face.

Joe followed her. "Need any help?"

"You can peel some potatoes if you want."

He'd never considered that he wanted to peel potatoes, but that afternoon he helped in the kitchen, enjoying himself.

His mother checked on them several times, smiling at their harmony but not interrupting. When Joe claimed part ownership in the cassoulet at dinner-time, she even backed up his claims, much to Ed's surprise.

"Oh, by the way, Joe," Ed added, "Luke's back. Seems he was on a mission somewhere down in Central America and got in trouble. Ricky Mercado helped save him and he's back."

"Good for him, Dad."

"Yeah, except that he's blind," Ed said with a heavy sigh.

"No!" Joe protested, concern in his voice. "Permanently?"

"They don't know. They say he's getting out, making the best of it. He always was a courageous man. I don't know that I'd do that well." Ed took a bite of his stew.

Joe continued to stare at his father.

Ginger leaned over to touch Joe's hand. "Is Luke a friend of yours?"

"More an acquaintance. He's a good man, though. The thought of him not being able to see— It's a horrible thought."

"I heard Mr. Mercado talking to his son on his cell phone on Wednesday. I think his son was still down wherever they were."

"Yeah, well, Luke and Ricky may be at the club tomorrow night," Ed said.

"Maybe we'll see them there," Joe said.

"You still going to let Ginger go?" Ed asked. "Aren't you worried about anyone trying to sneak her away?"

"No. I'll keep her at my side the entire time. We'll go by ourselves and then come back here late. I think we'll be all right. I've already talked to Justin about it and he assures me that the club will be secured."

Ginger sat quietly, listening to them discuss her life as if she didn't exist. But she trusted Joe.

"Okay with you, honey?" Joe asked.

"Okay with me. I can't wait to wear my blue gown. I've never had a dress like that." She knew it was a selfish reason, but she couldn't help herself.

"And you'll look beautiful," Vivian assured her.

The party had already begun when Joe and Ginger arrived at the country club Saturday night.

A crowd of the most important people in the country club was gathered by the door to the new Men's Grill to greet the guests. The two founding families were represented by patriarchs Archy Wainwright and Ford Carson, who didn't speak to each other but greeted partygoers. When Joe stepped in, Ginger's heart swelled with pride as everyone greeted him with acclaim.

With good reason. His design had improved the Men's Grill greatly. A young petite blonde stepped forward and kissed Joe's cheek, and Ginger stiffened.

"Jenny!" Joe exclaimed. "You look spectacular."

She did, and Ginger didn't like it one bit. She nudged Joe.

"Oh. I forgot you two hadn't met. Ginger, this is Jenny, the interior designer who worked with me on the Men's Grill. Jenny, this is my wife, Ginger Turner.''

Ginger stood tall and proud beside Joe, and Jenny stared in surprise.

"Joe, I had no idea you were married," she exclaimed.

"It's a recent development," he said, and leaned over to kiss Ginger's lips. Several people around them heard his remarks and word began to spread. The entire evening, they received congratulations from the membership. Joe kept his hand around Ginger's and towed her along for each introduction.

When she pointed out that she needed to be excused, he rounded up his mother and Amy and several other sisters-in-law to accompany her. Then he followed her to the rest-room door and waited for her to emerge.

"I'm safe, Joe," she whispered on the way back into the Men's Grill. "You don't have to stay beside me all evening. I can sit with your mother."

"You could, but I'd rather have you with me. You make me look good." He smiled down at her, and Ginger surrendered. He was too irresistible. Tomorrow she'd try to be more sacrificial. Tonight she was with Joe.

Once he and Ginger were safely in the car, Joe drove around the city, watching for anyone interested in their destination. He cleared his throat. "Uh, Mom asked permission to plan a party for us."

"I hate for her to go to that trouble," Ginger said

hesitantly. "By the time the party happened, we might have already passed the test for the INS."

"True, but even after we pass it, it doesn't mean we'll never see each other again. We'll have to stay married for at least a year."

"Yes, but…it seems so terrible to celebrate our scheme."

"Mom will enjoy having the party." He felt guilty, too, but part of his guilt was because of Ginger. His parents knew the reason for their marriage, but his mother still intended to make the marriage real. Ginger would be appalled if she knew that.

"If we had a party, people would bring us gifts and I'd feel so guilty." Ginger's blue eyes were wide in protest and Joe felt even worse.

"I know," he muttered. "But the problem is, Ginger, I can't really say no to my mother. She'd figure out something is wrong. Then she couldn't face the INS with honesty."

"You're right," Ginger agreed with a nod. "You've gone to a lot of trouble for me. I don't want you to think I'm not grateful."

Shooting her a quick smile, he said, "I know you are."

They drove in silence for several moments, both careful to watch for any familiar cars. Finally, Ginger spoke up.

"I scarcely got to visit with Daisy tonight, she was so busy."

"You miss spending time with her?"

"Yes."

"Why don't we take her out to dinner? If we go

to the club, it should be safe enough. Would Daisy mind going there?''

Ginger chuckled. ''It wouldn't be her first choice, but I'm sure she wouldn't. When could we go?''

''Tomorrow night would be good. Almost no one goes to the Empire Room on Sunday night because they're all there on Sunday after church. Want to call her in the morning?''

''Yes, Joe, thanks,'' she said, leaning over and kissing his cheek. ''You're so thoughtful.''

''Now, honey, most men wouldn't consider it thoughtful to agree to escort two beautiful women.''

''It won't be too dangerous to go out again?''

''I'll clear it with Justin and make sure we're safe. Just like tonight.'' He nodded his head and smiled, as if in appreciation and relief. ''It was a nice evening, wasn't it?''

''Yes, it was. And I loved wearing my new gown.''

''It looks great on you. My reputation shot through the roof once everyone knew you were with me.''

He reached over and held her hand in his as he drove with his left hand. He felt content.

''I saw a few women approving of you, too. Especially Jenny. She's very pretty.''

''Yeah. And she's talented. If I ever get started building the houses I want to build, I may ask her to do the interior design. It makes them easier to sell. Some people don't have the creativity to envision how the house can look when it's finished.''

Ginger kept her gaze down. "Maybe you should've married her," she said in a low voice.

After ensuring there was no one tailing them, Joe turned a back way into the alley behind his parents' house. "Ginger, I like Jenny, and she's pretty, but she's not the one for me. And I'm pretty sure she thinks I'm not the one for her. I can't exactly explain how that happens. But it does." He knew in his heart Ginger was the one for him. But he couldn't say that. It would freak Ginger out.

He shut off his headlights halfway down the alley. Then he pulled into his parents' garage and stopped the car. Quickly, he slipped from the car, met Ginger at the back of it and pulled shut the garage door.

He whispered into her ear, "In the house quickly."

Inside, Ed and Vivian were waiting for them. "We were worried about you two," Vivian said, reaching out to hug both of them.

"Thanks," Joe said. "We were just being cautious."

"Well, I'm glad you're home safely. It was such a lovely party, wasn't it?"

"Yes, it was. Thanks for coming."

Ed patted Joe on the shoulder. "We wouldn't have missed it, boy. We're very proud of you."

Ginger stood there, listening to their words, wondering if Joe had any idea how lucky he was. Her mother had never said those words to her. Never.

"And you, too, honey," Vivian said, hugging Ginger again.

"But I didn't do anything," she protested, surprised.

"That's not true, child," Ed said, beaming at her. "You looked beautiful and you had great manners. All the men were jealous."

Ginger thanked him and smiled, but she didn't believe him.

Vivian stuck her hand through Ginger's arm and started to the kitchen. "I've made a pot of decaf. Come in and let's discuss your wedding party. There were several things I had already thought about. Those crab puffs at the club were popular tonight. I think they'd be a good choice for the party."

Ginger looked over her shoulder at Joe, wondering how she should answer. When he shrugged, she said, "They were certainly good. It's one of the chef's new recipes."

"Are there others?" Vivian asked.

Ginger began naming some of the other recipes the chef had tried out on them. The club was trying to upgrade the quality of the food since they'd redone the Men's Grill.

They spent about half an hour in the kitchen. When Joe and Ginger rose to go upstairs, Joe added, "Oh, Mom, we're going out tomorrow night again. Ginger wants to see her friend Daisy. They haven't had a chance to visit since the incident Thursday."

"Oh, okay. In that case I'll get your dad to take me out, too." She nudged Ed, who rolled his eyes playfully.

"Yes, dear."

Upstairs, Ginger went into the bath first and Joe gathered up what he'd need in the bathroom after her.

She emerged looking just as beautiful in her nightgown and robe as she had in the evening gown. Joe struggled to keep his hands at his sides, glad he had to close the bathroom door between them as he went in.

Ginger finished putting her clothes away, then climbed into bed. But she didn't go to sleep. She wanted to ask Joe a question about the Wainwrights and the Carsons. She'd heard one of the Wainwright daughters had married one of the Carson men and wondered how the families could still be so distant, especially when a baby was on the way. She'd never before gone somewhere and then had the luxury of discussing things when she got home. And she knew Joe would indulge her.

As soon as he crawled under the covers, she began asking her questions, enjoying his responses and the several jokes he told her. She asked about one of the richest women in Mission Creek. "She wasn't wearing a very nice gown. Why?"

"Some wealthy people are spenders and some are stingy as hell. That lady acts like she's not going to eat the next day. But her money is all she has. I feel sorry for her."

"Me, too." She sighed. "The people in your life are more important."

"That's right." He slid his arm around her neck and pulled her closer for a kiss on the cheek. "Did your mother—'' He hesitated. ''I shouldn't ask that.''

''What?''

''Did your mother understand about the importance of people?''

''No. You're very fortunate to have such wonderful parents.''

''I know.''

They both lay silent. Then, unconsciously, she snuggled into Joe's arms and patted his shoulder. ''Very lucky indeed,'' she whispered.

Eleven

Excitement built in Ginger all day Sunday. Daisy was her only friend, and she couldn't wait to talk to her, though she wasn't sure how much Daisy would tell her with Joe present. Even though Daisy had told her about the baby, Ginger knew Daisy had more secrets she hadn't shared. But, then, Ginger hadn't told Daisy all her secrets, either.

That evening Ginger dressed in a casual skirt and jacket for dinner. It amazed her how quickly nice clothing gave her more confidence. She'd need to remember that when she'd have to live without Joe. Already, she had become greatly dependent upon him—which frightened her.

When she joined Joe downstairs to leave, he raised his brows in surprise. He held out his hand to take hers, but she ignored that action. It wasn't that she didn't want to hold his hand. She felt so safe, so loved, but she was misleading herself. It had to stop now.

"You okay, Ginger?" Joe asked.

She nodded her head and avoided his gaze. Then, since he still held out his hand, she gave in to his demand. A little smile glimmered across her lips. Joe was a determined man.

After they got in the car, they followed the roads to Daisy's modest apartment. Ginger knocked on the door and led her friend to the car.

Joe was friendly and receptive, as she'd hoped he would be. It was important to Ginger that Daisy like her husband, even if it wasn't a real marriage. Even if she knew those feelings were wrong.

At the club, the two women whispered to each other about how unusual it felt to be a guest where they worked.

Joe saw Justin across the room and excused himself to chat with him. Ginger was pleased since it gave her time for a private conversation with Daisy. She leaned closer to her friend.

"Daisy, have they found out anything about the baby?"

"No, but we're getting closer."

"But, Daisy, I think you should call the police."

"The police are involved, Ginger. This is a special situation. I'm going to get my baby back, I promise."

Ginger looked at the pain on her friend's face and hoped she was right. Daisy was a wonderful person and she deserved happiness.

As if Daisy read her mind, she said to Ginger, "I'm so happy for you. Joe seems like such a nice man."

"He is," Ginger said with a sigh. But Daisy didn't know that their marriage wasn't real, which meant the future held nothing but pain.

Joe came back to the table, smiling at both of

them. He was followed by the men who had caught his attention when they entered.

"Look, Ginger, it's Luke Callaghan and some friends. Did you meet him last night?"

Ginger shook her head, but she was distracted by a panic-stricken look on Daisy's face. Was something wrong?

Joe continued on without noticing Daisy's strained reaction. He took Ginger's hand and pulled her closer, putting her hand into Luke's and introducing her. Then he bent down and whispered into her ear, "He's blind, remember?"

"How do you do, Luke? I'm delighted to meet you."

Then she took Daisy's hand and placed it in Luke's. Daisy's cheeks flushed as if in a flash fire. "I'm—I'm…Daisy Parker," she stammered. An alert look came over Luke's face.

"Have we met before?" he asked.

"No," Daisy said fiercely.

"Are you sure? Your voice sounds familiar. Have you ever been to the Saddlebag?"

"No."

Ginger thought her friend was a little abrupt and hoped it didn't offend Luke. She noticed Joe was staring at Daisy also. Daisy pulled her hand away from Luke's and said, "I really need to go, Ginger."

Joe stepped closer to them.

"Are you sure, Daisy?" Joe asked. "Luke is about to tell us about his adventures in Central America."

Daisy stared at them. "Central America? No, no,

I can't stay. But I'll take a cab home. I don't want to mess up your evening.''

Joe shook his head. ''Nonsense, we'll catch up with Luke another time.''

Fortunately, they had met Daisy for an early dinner. Joe escorted them to the car and Daisy apologized several times for cutting their evening short.

''Don't worry about it,'' Joe said. ''This evening was planned for Ginger. She's missed seeing you.''

Once they were in the car, Joe asked her casually, ''You've never met Luke before?''

''No, I haven't.''

Ginger felt the tension in the air.

Desperate for a change of subject, she told her friend about Vivian's plans for a wedding party, hoping that would keep the topic of conversation from Luke. It did until they reached Daisy's apartment. Daisy got out, hugged Ginger goodbye and then hurried to her apartment. After they could see she was safely inside, Joe backed the car down the narrow drive and headed for his parents' home.

''Did you enjoy yourself?'' Joe asked, smiling at Ginger.

''I had a wonderful time, but I don't know why Daisy was so tense.''

''I don't, either, honey. But it's nothing to worry about.''

''But I wanted you to like Daisy.''

''I do.''

''Oh, good.''

The car phone rang as he turned into the alley. He snatched it up.

"Hello?"

"Joe, it's Justin."

"Yeah?"

"Where are you?"

"Entering the alley behind my parents' house."

"Have you seen a black limo tonight? The one Frank Del Brio uses when he wants to impress someone."

"No, why do you ask?"

"Frank's limo picked up three people at the airport tonight."

"Do you know who they were?"

"No, but I can guess. There was an older man, about your dad's age, a middle-aged man and a younger woman who looks a lot like your new bride. I suspect they'll try to make contact with her. Keep your eyes open and call if you need me."

Ginger had been watching Joe and realized the call meant there was trouble. But she didn't say anything until after they'd pulled into the garage and closed the door behind the car.

"Joe, what's wrong?"

"Later, honey. Once we're inside."

They hurried into the house, where Vivian and Ed were waiting for them. Ginger figured Joe wouldn't tell her anything until they were upstairs.

"I'm very tired," she said. "I think I'll go up and have my bath."

Joe leaned over and kissed her cheek, whispering in her ear, "I'll be right up."

That was what she wanted to hear.

That was what Joe wanted also. He needed a chance to warn his parents without Ginger hearing him. As soon as he heard the bedroom door close, he turned to his folks.

"Mom and Dad," he said quietly, "we've got problems."

Vivian's eyes widened. "What?"

"Ginger's mother and her stepfather are in town."

"Why is that bad? Won't Ginger be glad to see her mother?"

"Mom," Joe said in exasperation, "I told you her mother isn't like a regular mother. She's not here to help Ginger."

"Surely you don't think she'll hurt her?"

"Yes, I do. Keep her away from Ginger. Think you can do that?"

"Of course I can."

"I'll be here most of the day, but I have to go see about renting the office space I want. Justin will also be keeping an eye on things. I have to go upstairs and tell Ginger now."

"Oh, the poor child. It's going to be hard for her to hear that her mother will betray her," Ed said.

"It won't be a shock to Ginger, unfortunately."

Joe turned and hurried up the stairs, anxious to tell Ginger the bad news.

The bathroom door was still closed, but he could hear Ginger moving around. Hopefully she'd come out soon. He gathered his necessities for the bathroom, and when the door opened, he slipped in without waiting and closed the door behind him. He took a quick shower and came out again. Ginger was waiting by the door. She slipped into his arms, hers going around his neck. Joe drew a deep, scented breath; she smelled of flowers, youth, tenderness.

"What's wrong?" she whispered.

"Your mother's in town."

She jerked back, but he held her closer.

"Are you sure?"

"Yes, she's accompanied by two men. They sound like Leo and Harold."

Ginger hid her face in Joe's chest.

"Will they come get me?"

With a sigh, Joe said, "They'll probably try, but we're going to fight them. If they come to the house, stay up here. Mom won't tell them you're here."

"But I don't want to put her in danger."

"I'm sure they won't do anything to Mom. No one wants you to go. It's going to be all right. Justin will keep an eye on them."

He pulled back so he could see her face.

"Will you be all right?"

"Yes, of course."

They got into bed, but made no pretense of sleeping apart. Ginger snuggled up to Joe, needing the warmth of his body, his strength. After several moments of silence, she whispered, "Joe, do you remember when we talked about me being a virgin?"

"Yes."

"Don't you think it would be good if you made love to me now, in case they take me?"

Joe drew a deep breath. "Ginger, you're going to be all right. We're not going to let them take you. I told you that should be a special time with a special person."

"But, Joe—" Ginger began.

"I want you to wait. I want that time to be special. Now close your eyes and go to sleep. I'll keep you safe."

Joe prayed she did just that. He didn't think he could handle the temptation to take Ginger in his arms and make love to her as he wanted to. But that would be a betrayal of Ginger's trust. He couldn't do that.

He didn't relax until he heard Ginger's even breathing, telling him that she had gone to sleep. Thank God. Now he, too, could relax, knowing he'd need his rest for tomorrow. Tomorrow, when he'd have to make good on his promise to protect her.

The next day was tense. Of everyone, Ginger seemed the most calm. She sewed the baby blankets and read another mystery.

No one bothered them.

When the time came for Joe to meet the Realtor, he checked in with Justin.

"Can you keep an eye on those three while I check with the Realtor?"

"Of course," Justin assured him. "It's quiet around here."

Joe kissed his mother and Ginger goodbye, promising to be right back. He almost turned around and went back to the house, but he didn't want to miss his opportunity on this hot property. With determination, he got in his car and drove through the quiet streets of Mission Creek, keeping an eye open for the black limo.

When he reached the Realtor's office, he got out of the car and headed inside. Just as he put his hand on the door handle, the town erupted in a cacophony of sirens. Joe came to an abrupt halt and stared around him. What was going on? He rushed inside, pulling out his cell phone and calling Justin's private number. "Justin, what's going on?"

"I don't know. We've got a lot of crimes being called in. It could be something to distract us."

"Then I'm going back to the house."

He waved off the Realtor as he started toward him and then turned and ran out the door. He jumped into his car and rushed back toward his parents' home.

"What's going on?" Vivian asked as she walked into the den, the sound of the sirens ringing in her ears.

Ginger looked up and frowned. "Maybe there's an accident."

She was looking at Vivian as Vivian looked out the window. Tension filled Vivian's eyes.

"Ginger! The black limo! Get upstairs!"

She looked over her shoulder and caught a glimpse of her mother.

"Now, Ginger! Come on. I promised Joe."

Ginger moved toward the stairs, knowing she had to hide, but she wanted to face her mother. As she started up the stairs, she took Vivian's hand.

"Don't take any chances," she whispered. "Don't get hurt."

Vivian smiled and patted her hand. Sadly enough, though, Ginger believed her mother was capable of hurting anyone who got in her way. She moved up the stairs, but stayed close enough to the ground floor to be able to hear the conversation. A knock sounded on the door, and Vivian moved toward it.

"Can I help you?" Vivian asked in a pleasant voice.

"Hello," Ginger's mother snapped. "I wish to speak to Virvela Waltek."

Ginger could hear the puzzlement in Vivian's voice.

"I'm sorry. I don't know anyone by that name. Do they live in Mission Creek?"

"Yes, she married your son."

"Oh, you mean Ginger."

"Yes, I do. Where is she?"

"I don't know. They went on their honeymoon."

Ginger heard Vivian gasp and wondered what her mother had done.

"You are lying. Either produce her or I will kill you."

Ginger couldn't believe her mother's words.

"Mama, no!" she screamed, and sprang down the stairs, facing her mother for the first time in almost two years. Her mother, who held a small gun in her hand pointed at Vivian, chuckled, as if she'd pulled a good joke.

"Come quickly, Virvela. We do not have much time."

Helplessly, Ginger followed her mother from the house, after giving Vivian a swift hug.

"I'm glad you are reasonable, Virvela."

Actually, *scared* was more like it. She didn't doubt her mother would shoot Vivian. Not that Ginger was giving up. She had hidden her savings on her that morning, so that if she did get taken she might have a way of escaping. She had no intention of going with them quietly.

Her mother pulled open the door of the limo and shoved her in. She landed in a sprawl across the two men she least wanted to see. Harold helped her sit upright, but Leo let his hands linger. How she hated him.

Harold snapped, "To the airport, Dennis. And step on it. That bozo is already on his way back here."

Leo leaned back against the seat. "Who cares? We'll just shoot him. He doesn't matter."

"No!" Ginger exclaimed. "He's a good man. He doesn't deserve that."

"Be quiet," Leo growled.

When they got to the airport, Ginger noticed her mother putting her small gun in a pocket in the limo door.

"Aren't you taking the gun with you?" she asked curiously.

"Don't be silly. With all the restrictions today, I'd never make it. So we borrowed weapons for our trip."

Ginger sat back, thinking. So, once they were in the airport, they would have no firearms. She could walk away from them and they couldn't do anything. They didn't have a legal hold on her. There would be armed personnel in the airport who would protect her.

Suddenly, her future looked a lot brighter. She began hurriedly making plans. Once they left the limo, Ginger waited for her moment. When they reached the security gate, her mother shoved her toward the metal detector, but Ginger refused to walk through.

"Come through, miss," the guard ordered her.

"No, I'm not traveling today."

All three of her captors stared at her.

Harold, her stepfather, whispered in her ear, "Of course you are, or we'll go back and kill that woman."

Ginger knew this was the real test. Coolly, she stared at Harold.

"I can't stop you," she said affecting a careless tone in her voice, "but I won't even know because I'm not going back there. I'm going to another town, and this time I won't make the mistake of calling. But I will tell you this, that woman has five determined sons, and if you lay a hand on their mother they won't quit looking until they find you. Personally, I don't think she'd be worth the trouble. Besides, they've already identified all three of you."

She only prayed she was right.

"Damn you!" Leo said. "I don't know about that woman being worth the trouble, but you're definitely not. You're not even a virgin anymore."

Ginger smiled. In the distance, she heard the sound of sirens approaching.

"I think you better get on your plane right away," Ginger said, trying to look smug. "It sounds like the sheriff has arrived."

With a string of curses, Leo went through the security gates, followed by Harold and her mother. Her mother stopped once and turned back to face her.

"Don't ever come ask me for anything."

Ginger stared sadly at the woman.

"Don't worry, Mama. You have nothing I want." Then she turned and walked away, without ever looking back. Suddenly her heart leaped in her chest. There, coming down the concourse, was the one who had what she wanted. Joe. His arms were opened wide, a smile lit up his face. Racing toward him, she ran into his arms and his lips met hers.

"Where are they, baby?" Joe demanded against her lips.

"They're leaving," she said with laughter. "Leo doesn't want me anymore. After all," she said with a spreading grin, "I'm not a virgin anymore." Joe laughed and hugged her tighter.

"Come on, let's go tell Mom and Dad you're safe. They're worried about you."

Ginger looked at Justin, who had stood quietly off to the side. "Thanks for helping us."

"Ginger, I can stop them and have them arrested. All—"

Ginger held up a hand. "No, Justin. Just let them go. They didn't hurt anyone."

"How did you get away from them, anyway?" Joe asked.

"They told me they had to leave the guns here because of the metal detectors. They said they would go back and kill Vivian, but I didn't believe them. I told them there were five of you and you would get them if they hurt your mother."

"Well, you told the truth there."

"I know," she agreed with a smile. Then her expression sobered as she turned to the sheriff.

"Justin, do you think they're through with me? Or should I leave?"

"No," Joe said, rejecting her suggestion at once. "Where would you go?"

"Another small town, someplace they wouldn't look."

Joe pressed his mouth to her ear and whispered, "We have to live together to get your green card. They'd put me in jail if you left."

"They wouldn't really, would they?"

Justin watched them, not knowing what they were talking about.

"Didn't they say they would?" Joe whispered.

Ginger nodded. "Yes, but—"

"Then I reckon they would, Ginger."

"Oh."

Joe grinned at Justin, who was watching them. Out loud, he said, "Come on, honey. Let's go home. We'll work it out."

Joe took her hand in his and she felt safer than she had in months.

Twelve

Ginger wasn't surprised to find Vivian anxiously awaiting her return. She knew the generous woman was concerned about her safety.

"I am so sorry, Vivian. My mother—"

"I don't think she meant it, my dear."

"I hope she didn't," Ginger said, hanging her head. "But I can't be sure."

"But they left without you, right?"

"Yes. I guess. Leo decided I wasn't worth it," she said with a beaming smile.

"So they won't come back for you?"

"No, Leo doesn't want me anymore."

"Good, because Joe wants you," Vivian said.

Ginger smiled at her, but she didn't say anything.

At the sound of a car pulling up in front of the house, Joe leaned over to look out the window.

"It's Bill and Amy."

They got out of the car and hurried up the sidewalk. Vivian opened the front door.

"Did you hear?" she asked.

"Yes," her son replied. "Is everyone all right?"

"We're all fine. They're not going to chase after Ginger anymore. Joe and Justin scared them away."

"Mom, we didn't do anything," Joe said. "Ginger saved herself."

"Aha! Superwoman," Bill said with a grin.

Ginger's face turned bright red.

"Isn't it wonderful!" Vivian exclaimed. "Now our lives will be normal. We can settle down and have more grandbabies."

"Mom," Joe said in a warning voice. "Ginger wants to get her degree first."

"Oh, of course, dear. I'm so happy she wants to do that, but I hope it doesn't take too long. I think we should celebrate tonight. Ginger, would you make a cake? And, Amy, would you go call the others? Tell them we're having a celebration."

Ginger would have preferred a quiet evening, but if Vivian wanted to celebrate, then they would celebrate. She looked at Joe and shrugged her shoulders, then she started for the kitchen with Amy following her.

"Are you really okay with this?" Amy asked.

"Sure. I want Vivian to be happy. After all, my mother threatened to kill her."

Amy gasped. "You mean there really was a gun?"

"I'm afraid so."

"Wow! You'd better make it a chocolate cake."

"I agree," Ginger said, smiling.

"We better not mention that to the others. The boys are very protective of their mother."

"I know," Ginger agreed. "That's why they decided to leave without me." After a moment of silence, she asked, "Amy, may I ask you a question?"

"Yes, of course."

"Did you ask Bill to make love to you?"

Amy's eyes widened in surprise. "Uh, well, no, I—I mean I didn't have to ask. He convinced me."

With a sigh, Ginger said, "I knew it."

"Knew what?"

"I've already asked Joe twice, and he still isn't willing."

"He isn't? But I thought— You've already asked him twice?"

"Maybe I should ask him for a divorce."

"You want a divorce?"

"No, but— I'm still a virgin. Maybe I should ask Vivian for help. Because you can't have babies without, you know—"

"Oh, I can guarantee that one," Amy said with a grin.

Joe stuck his head inside the door. "Everything okay in here?"

Amy put her head down. "I think Ginger has some questions that you need to answer." She brushed past him at the door before he could stop her.

Joe looked at Ginger. "What's wrong?"

"Nothing's wrong," Ginger said, looking away from him.

"Then why did Amy say that?"

"I told her I was going to ask you for a divorce."

"A divorce?" he exclaimed, startled. "What are you talking about? We have to stay married for your green card." At the disappointed look on her face he asked, "That upsets you?"

"Well, it's just that— Well, Vivian wants us to have a baby."

Joe stared at her. "But you can't— We don't have to do that."

"I know. But…it's very confusing. I feel like I'm cheating Vivian."

"Honey, we got married for you to become a citizen. But I promised you I wouldn't make love to you."

"But you didn't tell Vivian that."

"Remember when I said we wouldn't change your virgin status?" Joe cleared his throat. "You want me to tell Mom that we're not going to stay married?"

"No!" Ginger said, her voice rising in protest.

"But, Ginger, if you have my baby, I'm not going to let you divorce me."

"Oh," she said, as if she suddenly understood.

Which was more than Joe did.

After a moment of silence, he said, "I wasn't going to marry, because I was never going to face divorce. I was never going to split up my family."

"But, Joe, we would have a divorce no matter what."

"No, because I didn't really count this a marriage."

"But we got married."

"True, but we both knew it wasn't real, remember?"

"I'm very confused," Ginger said, protest clear in her voice.

"Damn it, you think *you're* confused? Do you want to stay married?"

"It will upset Vivian if we get a divorce."

"So you want to stay married to me because of Mom? That doesn't make sense, Ginger."

"Yes, it does. You have a wonderful mother. And family. They don't deserve to be hurt. You know, I've been thinking about the bakery shop."

"What bakery shop?" He looked totally confused by her abrupt change of subject.

"Your father said I could make a lot of money with a cinnamon bun shop. Then I could pay my own way. And if I had babies, I could hire someone to help and keep earning money, and people wouldn't say I was marrying you for your money."

"Who said such a ridiculous thing?"

She looked away. "There's been talk."

"Well, it's ridiculous. I would be the lucky one if we married."

"We don't have to marry. We are married."

"I know that!"

Vivian stuck her head through the door. "Are you two fighting?"

"No," he snapped.

"Yes," Ginger said softly.

"And it's your fault, Mom," Joe complained.

"What?"

"Never mind. This is the craziest conversation I've ever had."

"But, Joe—" Ginger protested.

"No more discussion now. We'll talk later, when we're alone."

"Well, since you're going to save your discussion," Vivian said, "the rest of the family has arrived, so come on out. Let's all celebrate."

Ginger left the room with Vivian.

Joe stood there, staring after them. He'd be glad to celebrate.

If he knew what the hell he was celebrating.

Ginger's hands were shaking later when she tried to cut the cake. She sent a silent plea to Amy, who with understanding quickly stepped to her side and reached out for the knife.

"I think Vivian forgot the napkins, Ginger," she said, giving Ginger an excuse to get away and compose herself.

"I'll get some," Ginger said gratefully as she saw Joe enter the room, leaving the kitchen empty. She certainly didn't want to face him again, alone. She slipped into the kitchen just as he turned to look for her. She realized she'd made a mistake. Joe didn't understand what she was hinting at. He didn't understand her past, in her country.

In Estonia, she'd been in a poverty-stricken neighborhood. Many marriages took place but most were not a love match. People married for financial reasons, or because of children. Ginger had been attracted to Joe because of his manners, the way he treated women, his place in society. Since he'd married her, taken her under his wing, she'd discovered more reasons. When he held her at night, she felt safe, treasured, even desired, though it was obvious she was mistaken in that.

She wanted Joe to make love to her. She wanted Joe to father her child. He was an honorable man, a father a child could respect, admire, honor. Even if Joe didn't want to stay married to her, she knew Joe would not abandon his child. And she would be able to support her child, especially if she had her own business.

In her neighborhood those would all be good reasons, she knew. But she didn't live there anymore. Coupled with desire, many a marriage had lasted entire lives. But without desire, they didn't do so well. What about her and Joe? Was there desire between them? Twice she'd tried to convince him to take her, to see if he felt anything, but he didn't. What did that tell her?

And would she listen?

Rousing herself from contemplation, she came back with the napkins.

"Are you all right, dear?" Vivian asked, taking hold of her hand. "Amy said your hands were shaking."

"Delayed reaction, Vivian, that's all. I would never forgive myself if I ever hurt you." She hugged Vivian. Suddenly Joe was beside the two of them.

"You risked your life to save Mother," Joe said. "You have nothing to blame yourself for."

"Thank you, Ginger," one of the younger brothers

called out. "In case we all didn't say it before, we're very grateful."

Ginger wanted to roll up into a ball and hide herself. Trying to deflect their praise, she said, "I can't take all the credit, you know. I told them about Vivian's five ferocious sons, and they gave up on me."

The men cheered and pumped up their muscles to prove how frightening they might be if anyone bothered their mother.

After they settled down, the family lounged in the living room for several hours. Toward the end of the evening, someone asked Joe if he and Ginger were moving back to his condo.

"Not this evening, as long as Mom and Dad don't mind. We'll sleep here tonight and move back to the condo tomorrow." He paused and then looked at Ginger. "If that's all right with you, Ginger."

Like a dutiful wife, Ginger nodded and agreed at once.

Amy gathered up the dirty dishes and started carrying them to the kitchen. She persuaded her husband to help her, but they were talking more than they were working, Ginger noticed. She hoped Amy wasn't divulging what Ginger had shared with her earlier.

Some of the younger brothers teased Bill about doing women's work, but it didn't faze him. He pointed out that his brothers should learn the benefit of shared work. With a wicked look at his trim, beautiful wife, he conveyed his meaning quite clearly.

Amy giggled like a carefree teenager as the other men jumped up to offer their belated assistance.

Ginger felt relieved until she saw Bill draw Joe to one side. Then she scurried up to bed, telling Vivian and Ed she was tired. She wanted to be in bed with her eyes closed before Joe came upstairs.

"What is it?" Joe asked as Bill motioned him outside.

"Nothing," Bill said casually, but he kept pulling him farther into the shadows.

Joe waited. Bill led him around to the side of their childhood home. Then he stopped. "Joe, do you need to talk about something?"

He and Bill had been the two oldest. They'd shared a lot as children. "Amy told me you and Ginger have problems."

Joe's eyes widened. "No! I mean, if it was what happened today, it was nothing. Ginger was shaken up by the events and she hated that you all thought her mother would hurt Mom."

"No, this was personal about you and Ginger." Bill swallowed hard, obviously uncomfortable. "Look, Joe, I'll admit I didn't understand what Amy tried to tell me, but...you do still like women, don't you?"

Joe groaned. "Yes, I do, and my wife is at the top of that list."

He blew out a breath. "I thought so. She's a cute little thing."

"Yeah. Say, Bill, do you know who owns that empty storefront on the town square?"

Since Bill's law office was located downtown, he knew about the property and its owner, Fred Gunther, and was able to give Joe a few details. When Joe explained Ginger's dream, Bill was excited about the idea. "Have you tasted her cinnamon rolls?"

"Yeah," Joe said with a nod. "They're real good."

"As good as the club's?"

"Ten times as good. She'd win that contest hands down."

"Great! Want me to talk to Fred? Since his Molly died, he hasn't shown much interest in anything."

"Not yet. Ginger just came up with this idea recently and we've had a lot on our minds the last few days."

"I guess so. Let me know when I can help you." He clapped Joe on the shoulder and headed to the car where Amy and their children waited for him.

Joe headed for the stairs after telling his parents good-night.

Much to his relief, Ginger had already fallen asleep. He wasn't up to a serious discussion about their future tonight. But since she was asleep, he could hold her close for tonight and enjoy her warmth. For just a little while.

Ginger slipped out of the room the next morning while Joe was still sleeping. She had to force herself to do so, but she was more depressed than she'd been since she'd married Joe. She had no hope now that he'd want to keep her. She knew now that he had no desire for her. None.

In the kitchen she again made up a batch of cinnamon buns. As the mouthwatering scent made its way up the stairs, she heard someone stirring. She tried not to show her disappointment when Joe's parents appeared. She'd hoped the first down would be her husband.

"Are you sure you don't want to stay here with us?" Ed asked, a big smile on his face.

"Sorry, Ed. I can't do that. The lady who taught me to make these said I should use them to catch a husband. She said a light hand with pastry is a gift and can't be taught."

"Good thing Joe caught you before anyone here knew about your buns," Ed said. "At least I get some every once in a while."

"You're right, Dad. Good morning," Joe said, bending over to kiss Ginger's cheek. "Did you sleep well?"

"Of course she did. All her worries are over!" Vivian said, beaming at them.

"Well, maybe not all her troubles, Mom. We still have the test for the INS," Joe reminded her.

"That can't be a problem," Vivian protested.

"Now, honey," Ed cautioned gently.

"Well, it can't, Ed. It's obvious to all of us that they love each other. When will they interview you?"

"I don't know," Joe replied. "They said they'd call, but I haven't heard from them."

"I hope it's soon," Vivian said.

"It really doesn't matter," Joe said, as if he really meant it.

Ginger jumped up from the table. "I'll go start to pack," she said, and slipped from the kitchen.

"Mom, we'd better not discuss everything so openly in front of Ginger. I don't think she's used to that."

"Probably not, but don't you think she should get used to it?"

"She will. She's very bright. I'll go help Ginger pack."

He stood to join Ginger.

"Honey, do you think she'll want to take these leftover buns with her?" Vivian asked as Ed moved a step closer to the table, an eager look in his eyes.

"I guess we can split them, Mom. I don't suppose they'll be as good after this morning."

"But Ginger said they don't waste anything in her neighborhood because everyone is so poor. The second day, they would take the leftovers and fry them in butter. She said they were even better that way."

"Yeah, let's split them!" Ed agreed.

Joe tried to hold back his smile. He could even admit to wanting to taste day-old cinnamon rolls. For research, of course. But first he and Ginger had to get back to their condo and put their life in order.

They said their goodbyes, with a few tears from the ladies. Then five minutes later, they were back in their condo, each having carried in a load of their belongings.

Ginger took two bags to their bedroom, while he took a sack of groceries to the kitchen. Vivian had been afraid they would starve before they had time to do any shopping.

"Joe, you have messages," he heard Ginger call from the bedroom.

"Play them," he replied as he placed the perishables in the refrigerator.

She backed away. "No. They won't be for me."

He laughed as he made his way to the room. Pencil and paper in hand, he played the messages. "Joe, it's Mr. Cooper. Give me a call. I want to build a house for my son and his new wife. Your dad said you'd consider doing a house."

Joe looked pleased, Ginger noted. Perhaps he had his first new client.

There were several other calls from people she didn't know. Then came a voice she recognized. "Mr. Turner, this is Mr. Fisher of the INS. We've scheduled your interview for Tuesday, April 9, at 11:00 a.m. If I don't hear from you, we'll assume that date is satisfactory."

"Today?" Ginger screamed. "They're coming today? B-but we're not ready!"

Joe stared at his watch. "I'm afraid it's a little late to protest. They'll be here in fifteen minutes."

Thirteen

Ginger turned shocked eyes to Joe. "Now? They're coming now?"

"It's okay, Ginger," Joe reassured her. "We'll explain what happened." Though they were running rampant, he was trying to collect his thoughts. Everything would turn out okay, he told himself. He simply would accept nothing less. "Just stay calm."

"Yes, but we haven't— I mean, isn't it necessary to—"

"Make love? I don't think so. We've slept with each other, you know. Just because we haven't been intimate right away doesn't mean we aren't going to stay together unless— That is what you still want, isn't it?"

He knew he was asking for a commitment from her, but after all, he had committed himself to this so-called marriage.

Ginger stared at him as if struggling to make a decision. Her gaze circled the room. Then she gave him a brief nod, as if her decision had been made, and she hurried to the door.

"It will be all right, Ginger," Joe said once more, as if saying so would make it true.

* * *

Ginger had made her decision. There was no point in doing anything halfway. An old friend had told her that. So, until the INS men left Mission Creek, she was truly married to Joe Turner—exactly as she dreamed each night.

There wasn't much time but there was no hesitation. She was dressed in a casual dress that flattered her. All she added was an apron taken from her kitchen drawer. She tied it around her trim waist and began taking down a big mixing bowl and the ingredients for her cinnamon rolls.

She quickly prepared the coffeepot and plugged it in, then began making the dough for the rolls. Gretta, an old woman from her village, had told her the scent drew men like bears to honey. Gretta was a sturdy woman, gentle and kind, but not particularly beautiful. Yet she'd buried four husbands.

For years Ginger had worked in Gretta's market and bakery. When Ginger's mother had found it inconvenient to have her come home late at night, she'd slept in Gretta's storeroom until 4:00 a.m., when Gretta woke her to start the morning baking. The old woman taught her about life as well as baking.

In that moment in Joe's bedroom, Ginger had determined to commit herself to this marriage, however long it lasted. She would fight for her marriage…with cinnamon buns.

Joe watched Ginger leave him. What had that look meant? She'd suddenly seemed calm. That was good.

He thought it was good. Unless she'd decided to confess all to the INS men.

He straightened his shoulders, like a soldier going into war. He hoped not. He wanted to remain married to Ginger. He wanted to protect her, keep her safe. More than that, he wanted her to have the right to make choices for her life. To have the opportunities most kids in Mission Creek took for granted.

The age business still bothered him, but when he'd mentioned it to Ginger, she didn't seem to make much of it. He'd decided not to make a big deal of it, either.

A knock at the door told him his time for contemplation had just run out. He drew a deep breath and marched across the living room, hearing Ginger in the kitchen, and opened the door.

Carl Fisher and Craig Caldwell stood outside the door, waiting. "Good morning, Mr. Turner. May we come in?"

"Of course," he murmured. Before any of them could speak, Ginger called from the doorway.

"Come in, gentlemen. May we talk in the breakfast room while I work? I'm doing some baking."

Joe figured the men would agree. When Ginger gave her best smile, few men would turn her down. Besides, something smelled good.

"Of course, Mrs. Turner," Fisher agreed, as Joe had expected.

As Joe followed the other two men to the kitchen, he wondered why Ginger had suddenly decided to begin baking.

"I hope you don't mind if I continue to work. I promised Joe's mama I'd make some of my cinnamon buns for a bake sale."

"Not at all," Fisher said. "So, you're getting involved with the community?"

"Not exactly. We've had a little difficulty to start off our marriage, as my husband will tell you. Right, dear?" She turned to Joe and reached up to lightly brush his lips with hers.

Joe grabbed for his chair, hoping he could get seated before he fell forward on his face. He'd dreamed of Ginger like this, a real wife, accepting of his caresses. He hadn't gone so far as to dream of *her* offering caresses to *him*.

Fisher's look toward him wasn't nearly as gentle as his looks to Ginger, but Joe understood. "There were several attempts to kidnap Ginger by a couple of local hoods."

Ginger began pouring rich, fragrant coffee into cups she had apparently set out before their arrival. Fisher was distracted from Joe's words. "That's not necessary, Mrs. Turner."

"Only if you do not care for coffee, Mr. Fisher," Ginger said, giving him another beautiful smile. "But I promise you this is special coffee."

Fisher's approval was obvious for anyone to see. In fact, Joe was a little irritated by the man's approval of Ginger. He cleared his throat. "Uh, thank you, Mrs. Turner, I'd be glad to share a cup." Then he turned to Joe. "Kidnappers? Surely you exaggerate, Mr. Turner."

That really irritated Joe. He drawled, "I thought so myself, Mr. Fisher. But I consulted my friend, Sheriff Wainwright. He advised me to be careful. Two days later, when I caught the same two men with a handkerchief soaked in ether dragging my wife to a car left running, I became a believer."

Even thinking about their treatment of Ginger upset him and his voice rose. Soft, warm arms slid around his shoulders and Ginger kissed his cheek. "My husband was a true hero," Ginger assured them. Her touch soothed Joe, too.

"You were pretty heroic yourself, Ginger," he said more easily. "She bit the man with the ether before it could take its desired effect," Joe told them proudly.

With admiration on his face, for Ginger, Joe knew, Fisher said, "That must have been difficult, Mrs. Turner."

"To keep her safe, we moved to my parents' house. She gave up her classes and work, places they would expect her to be."

"We're glad you took precautions," Fisher said with a nod. "Now—"

"They found her, anyway," Joe added, almost casually, setting them up for the finale. He didn't like their attitude.

"They? The two hooligans?" Caldwell asked in surprise.

"No. Her mother, her husband, and the old man they wanted her to marry. They kidnapped her, took her to the airport, planning on taking her back to

New York City. Her mother pulled a gun on my mother and threatened to kill her if Ginger didn't go with them.''

Ginger had gone back to the kitchen counter, rolling out some dough. She was making a quick version of the buns. It wasn't quite as good as the original, but she needed rolls ready soon. She looked up and nodded sadly when the men stared at her. ''It's true. I was horrified, worried for my mother-in-law's safety.''

The two men looked back to Joe, now caught up in the story. ''What happened?'' Fisher asked.

''I called the sheriff and chased after them, but Ginger is the hero. She escaped from them. You explain, Ginger.''

''When I realized they could not take their guns through Security, I made a scene and walked away from them.'' She slid smaller versions of the rolls into the oven, then she straightened. ''Besides, the man wanted a virgin.'' She shrugged and grinned. ''Instead, I am a married woman now.''

She again slid her arms around Joe's shoulders and this time kissed the top of his head.

''You know, I think we may not have to wait the year to get you your green card. You've been working here for two years already and—''

The phone rang and Joe got up to answer it. Carl Fisher stopped talking.

''No, I can't,'' Joe said to the caller.

After a pause and an obvious argument, Joe repeated, ''I can't.''

Ginger went to his side and mouthed, "What is it, Joe?"

He put a hand over the mouthpiece of the phone. "It's the mayor. He's called a sudden meeting about that government project I was telling you about."

"Oh, Joe, you've got to go. It would mean so much to the start of your new business." She turned to their guests. "Gentlemen, you do understand, don't you? You can talk to me and meet with Joe later, couldn't you?" she pleaded.

"Yes, of course," Fisher agreed. Joe figured he would have agreed to anything if Ginger asked it.

"It won't affect the outcome?" he asked warily.

"Not at all."

Joe hesitated, but then the mayor urged him once again to come immediately. He agreed reluctantly, then hung up the phone and swept Ginger into his embrace. "You're sure you don't mind?"

"Of course not."

He kissed her goodbye, only in pretense for the INS men, he told himself, and hurried out the door.

Ginger turned to the two men. "Thank you for being so considerate. Joe is moving his work from Chicago to Mission Creek. We both prefer it here."

"I'm happy to hear that. But as I was saying, I think the government might agree to consider you abused. A woman abused by her husband can leave him and still receive her green card. I think that your mother's abuse of you, as you're still technically a child would count the same. You could still get the green card for your marriage, but you can get it more quickly this way. Not waiting for a year."

"Truly?" Ginger asked, afraid to breathe. "And I can stay forever?"

"Forever," Fisher agreed solemnly and then broke into a smile when she burst into tears. "Here, now. No need to cry."

The oven buzzed, distracting Ginger. She pulled the rolls, now a tender brown and smelling heavenly, out of the oven and put them on top of the stove. "You must taste my rolls to celebrate!" she exclaimed. She dished one on each saucer and put them before the men. Then she refilled their coffee cups. Joining them at the table, she listened to every detail.

After the men left, Ginger cleaned the kitchen, her heart filled with joy. She would be an American for life. She could apply for her citizenship. Her dream had come true because of Joe. She owed it all to him. Left on her own, she would have run and been in hiding the rest of her life.

But would Joe see that? Would he send her back to her apartment if he thought living with him wasn't necessary? She froze at that thought. She didn't want to leave Joe. She could convince him. She could! Gretta had taught her how to please a man. Oh, not in bed. Gretta had said that was the easy way. The hard way was to go with your emotions. Show him he was the most important person in the world to you.

Joe *was* the most important man in the world. She would not care about staying in America without him. So what should she do? If only she didn't need to tell him. She could— She gasped. Could she do such a devious thing?

To achieve happiness with Joe, she could.

She would stay in Joe's condo and try to convince him that she was important to him, too. She could contribute to their marriage in many ways. But she wouldn't use sex to tempt him. That wouldn't be fair. It was bad enough that she was keeping the truth from him. She would show him life together could be good. Yes, that was what she'd do.

Joe drove a little too fast on his return to the condo. He'd been gone a little more than an hour, but he had good news. He'd gotten the job, but what would that mean to him if he lost Ginger? He'd planned on throwing himself on the mercy of the law if they tried to send her away.

He checked the windows of his condo, afraid he'd see them dark and empty. But the lights were on and he held his breath. Surely that meant Ginger was still there. They wouldn't have taken her away until he got back, would they? He parked in a hurry and jumped out of the car. He rushed into the building to his apartment and pushed open the door, noting that it wasn't locked. "Ginger?"

"Here, Joe," she said, poking her head out of the kitchen.

"Where are the government men? Are they still here?"

"No. They said this obviously was a bad time and

there was no rush. They would be in contact later.'' She smiled at him. "How did the meeting go?''

"Great. But they didn't threaten you, or say you'd have to come back to their office?''

"No, not at all. They were very nice. They said we had at least a year. That's what you said earlier, isn't it? They said they'd call us. Now, pull out a chair and tell me all about your meeting.''

Joe felt a little dazed as he sat down. He'd been worrying the entire time he was gone. He'd been anxious for the government work, but he found it didn't mean nearly as much as Ginger's safety and whether or not Ginger got to stay. "Uh, they liked my plan. Good thing I'd prepared for it.''

Ginger threw her arms around his neck and kissed his cheek. He squeezed her tight and thought yes, it was a good thing, now that he was home with Ginger.

Joe sat down to a terrific dinner. Not that Ginger did all the work. He helped out. They made it together. While they did, she chatted about how nice it was to be in their own home. But she quickly added how much she loved his mother and father.

During dinner they talked about his plans again for the development he was going to work on.

"Will you make enough to cover your expenses, or will you need to find more jobs, too?''

"I'll make enough for several years, honey. I told you they pay architects a lot here. Is there something you want?'' She'd never asked for anything specifically, but he didn't want his wife lacking for anything.

She stared at him, a startled expression on her face. "Me? Want something? No, I was trying to be subtle," she said, a rueful expression on her face. "I want to—to use my savings, but if we need it to buy, I don't have to—to spend it. I can put it in the bank."

Ginger stood and began clearing the table. He immediately helped her. Following her into the kitchen, he blocked her way as she turned to go back to the dining room. "What are you talking about, Ginger? What are you wanting to do?"

She shot him a quick look and then turned away. "Um, I had that idea to open a shop and sell my cinnamon buns. I could make some money."

"That would be a lot of work, Ginger. I can make plenty of money for us, I promise."

"But you shouldn't have to pay for me. I can work and still go to school. Now that I don't have to worry about calling attention to myself, I can start a business. I have my savings."

"How much savings do you have?" he asked. He figured she didn't know how much she'd need. Maybe he could help her without her knowing.

"I have a little over ten thousand. I think I can rent a space, make a few purchases and still have a little left over."

"If you're serving food, you have to meet certain health standards."

"I know the rules. I have been hoping to do this since I ran away from home, but I was afraid it would draw too much attention to me and the police would make me go back to New York.''

"But I want you to have time to shop or go out with friends. A business would require a lot of time.''

"You will be working, won't you? So I should work.''

"Amy doesn't work.''

"No, but she takes care of the children. We have no children.''

Had she read his mind? He'd been thinking about sex ever since he began sharing a bed with Ginger. Now that their problem with the INS had been postponed, he'd been thinking about tonight. When Ginger got in his bed tonight, he'd thought it might be a good time to discuss changing their relationship, taking it to the next level. But her mind was on making money.

"Uh, well, we can talk about your business idea later, in a week or two, after you've had some rest. Things have been kind of hectic since we got married.''

"In Estonia, the women work as hard as the men. You aren't taking a few weeks off, are you?''

"Of course not! The government wants me to start working on the project at once. I've got to present preliminary plans in three months. I'm going to have to work overtime to make that deadline.''

"If I'm busy working, I won't be disturbing you. And I will make more money for us. Sometimes in Estonia, the government demands things, but they don't always pay on time. We might need extra money.''

He raked his hand through his hair. "Maybe you should discuss this idea with my mom. She might be able to explain things better than I.''

"Of course. I'll go see her in the morning while you're working.''

"Damn, I haven't started teaching you how to drive. I'll have to drop you off. But then I'll have to take you home. Maybe I can talk to Mom and she'll drive you home." He reached for the phone.

Her hand landed on top of his. "Do not worry about it. I'll arrange everything." She smiled a sweet smile that made him more anxious for bedtime.

She stood. "I'm going to take a bath tonight. I missed the tub while I was at your parents'.''

"Of course," he agreed. He clicked on the television. "One of my favorite shows is coming on now.''

"Good. Would you like a cup of decaf before I go?''

He grinned. "Yeah, that would be great." In no time, he had his feet up, the television on and a cup of coffee beside him. Ah, married life.

Married life stopped being so wonderful when Ginger stepped back into the den. She looked beautiful and smelled great when she leaned over him and picked up the coffee cup. Joe wanted to bury his face in her hair and pull her against him.

Instead, she headed for the kitchen. When she

came back she asked what time he wanted breakfast. That was better. "I'll need to get to work about eight, so why don't we have breakfast together at seven-thirty. Is that okay with you?"

Ginger said that would be fine. Before Joe could suggest going to bed, she leaned down, kissed his cheek and said good-night. Then she headed for the bedroom she'd used that first night.

"Where are you going?" he asked.

She appeared startled. "To bed."

"But I thought we'd sort of gotten used to sharing the same bed."

"But my mother doesn't want me anymore, Joe. I'm perfectly safe here with you. I'm not scared anymore."

"Oh, I see. Are you sure?"

"You're teasing me, aren't you?" she said with a chuckle. Then she gave his cheek another kiss and walked into her bedroom.

He sat there staring at the closed door. This wasn't what he thought would happen tonight. Where had he gone wrong? He thought he'd had everything planned out. Maybe he needed to talk to Bill or his dad. This married stuff might be a little more complicated than he'd thought.

Fourteen

Ginger made another delicious breakfast for Joe the next morning. Then, as soon as she escorted him out the door with a kiss goodbye that made her want to return to bed—this time with Joe—she picked up the phone and called Vivian. "Hi, it's Ginger. May I come talk to you?"

Vivian's voice came singing through the wires. "Of course you can. I've been dying to call you, but Ed said I should give you some space."

"Joe said I should talk to you. I'll be there in about twenty minutes." After all, she had to walk.

When she reached Vivian and Ed's house, there were several cars parked out front. Was Vivian having company?

Vivian swung open the door. "What took you so long? I thought maybe you'd changed your mind."

"No, and I walked as fast as I could but—"

"Walked?" Amy asked, coming into the room. "You walked all the way from Joe's condo to Mom's house?"

Several others filed into the room, a look of horror on their faces.

"I hope you don't mind, but I invited the rest of

my daughters to have coffee with us," Vivian said as three more ladies followed Amy.

"Of course I don't mind, but I thought they were…" She stared at all the wives of her husband's brothers.

Vivian laughed. "Married to my sons? They are, but I wanted a little girl so badly that they allow me to call them my daughters. Would that bother you?"

"I'd be delighted, Vivian. Could I call you Mom?"

"I'd love it, dear." She took Ginger by the arm and drew her to the living room where a tray of coffee and cookies awaited her arrival. Everyone sat down, pleasure on their faces.

Ginger, her hand in Vivian's, suddenly pulled back. "Maybe I shouldn't take that liberty until—" She stopped abruptly, slapping a hand over her mouth.

Everyone stared at her, but it was Amy who wanted to know why she should wait and what she should wait for.

Ginger hesitated, but there seemed no reason for secrecy now. Everyone's ears perked up and they exchanged several glances before all their gazes concentrated on Ginger.

"Why, dear, whatever do you mean?" Vivian asked.

"I meant, maybe I shouldn't call you Mom until… You see, Joe and I aren't really married."

All the oxygen was suddenly sucked out of the air.

"Oh, no!" Kitty complained. "That means I lost my bet with Rodney."

"What bet?" Amy asked.

"I bet him my new gold bracelet that Joe would marry before the next grandbaby was born." Several ladies laughed. One of them pointed out, "Since you were the one carrying the baby, didn't Rodney think you had an unfair advantage?"

"No, because when we made the bet, I wasn't pregnant." The rueful look on her face drew more laughter.

"You won your bet, darling," Vivian said calmly. "I saw the certificate with my own eyes. And Joe looked into my eyes and told me they were married. He never could lie to me."

"Good," Kitty said, smiling. "'Cause I love my bracelet."

Amy stopped the celebrating. "But if you're married, Ginger, why did you say that?"

Without hesitation, she said, "Because we have not been intimate. And so we can't make babies. So I shouldn't call her Mom when there's no possibility of having babies."

"Why?" one of the women asked. "You get married so you don't have to sneak around. Doing it is legal then!"

Ginger shook her head. "No, we got married for my green card."

All the ladies began talking, commenting on what had happened and whether or not they would have done the same. Several of them asked questions about Ginger's life and her family.

Vivian quickly defended her. "Her mother is the one who threatened to shoot me if Ginger didn't go back with her and marry a fifty-eight-year-old man. Doesn't that tell you something?"

"So you asked Joe to marry you so you wouldn't have to go back?"

Feeling a little embarrassed, Ginger said, "Not exactly. I had planned to run away. I was trying to escape when Joe found me."

Silence fell around the room as everyone stared at Ginger. She figured her story would shock them. "I know I shouldn't have but—"

"You mean," Amy said, choosing each word carefully, "you mean *Joe* is the one who offered marriage?"

To Ginger's mind, they all stared at her as if she'd accomplished some miracle. She looked at each one of them carefully. "He didn't exactly offer it. He stared at me funny and then told the officers that we were running away to Las Vegas to marry the next day."

Vivian reached over to hug her, tears in her eyes. "Oh, thank God! My prayers have been answered!"

Though Ginger returned Vivian's hug, she didn't understand. "What is it, Vivian? What did you pray for?"

"You, my child. I prayed for you."

Bewildered, Ginger looked at Amy. "What does she mean?"

"We all wanted Joe to be happy, to find someone he could love, but he resisted."

"Yeah, I brought all my college friends here to meet Joe," Kitty said, "and they adored him. But he never even saw them."

The other wives told similar tales. Ginger didn't get the significance of them.

"But if he did not love them…"

"That's just it, Ginger. He must love you!" Amy said with a beaming smile.

Ginger felt a similar smile blooming inside her and she wanted to believe them. But she knew better. "Oh…no." Then reality took over. "No, he does not love me like—like that."

"Why do you say that?" Amy asked.

Highly embarrassed by the question, she finally said, "I offered to—to let him…and he refused. He would not." She shrugged her shoulders, as if it was a hopeless cause.

Quiet fell again, then Vivian asked her, "How did he say no? Did he say he was too busy?"

"No. He said it would not be right. He said he was too old. He said he wanted it to be special for me. That one day I would meet someone…" She let her voice fade away.

Kitty asked softly, "And you didn't tell him you already had?"

Ginger shook her head, understanding exactly what Kitty was suggesting. Then she realized what she was admitting and she froze. "No! No, I mean, uh, I—"

Amy caught Ginger's hand. "It's okay to admit it, we've all gone through the same thing," she said softly. "The Turner boys are pretty potent." Everyone's eyes turned to Vivian.

"Don't look at me. Their dad was no slowpoke, either," she explained with a laugh.

"But he doesn't love me," Ginger said mournfully.

"Oh, yes, he does," Vivian countered. "My sons are gentlemen, but they're not martyrs. He loves you. He just told you he loves you more than he loves sex itself. And for a man like him, that's the most loving thing he can do, exclude himself from great pleasure to make life better for you."

"How romantic," Kitty said with a sigh. "It's just what Rodney would do."

Rodney was the youngest and less mature than the others and Ginger expected to hear protests from the other ladies, but they were all smiling softly and nodding.

Again, she was almost swept away in agreement. Until she remembered. "No, no, I wish he was, but you don't understand. He's going to divorce me after a year. He's said that often."

"So you won't get your green card for a year?" one of the women asked.

She'd lied to her husband, but she couldn't lie here. She just couldn't. "That's what I told him," she said, staring at her hands twisted together in her lap.

"Isn't it true? I mean, Joe's not dumb. He checks things out," Vivian assured her.

"I know. But the agents discovered what my mother had done and are allowing me to get my green card because they say my mother abused me."

The others congratulated her. Then Vivian asked the question she was dreading.

"Why haven't you told Joe that?"

In a whisper, Ginger said, "I don't want to leave him. I thought if I didn't tell him, I'd have a year to try to persuade him to love me."

She expected to be condemned by the other wives and her mother-in-law for lying to the man she loved. Instead, several of them said, "Good thinking."

"But I'm lying to him," she pointed out.

Vivian nodded. "Sometimes you have to, dear." She began pouring coffee and passing around cups and urging everyone to test the cookies. Then she leaned forward and said, "Okay, what's your plan?"

Her idea of starting a business, selling her cinnamon rolls, got a lot of approval…but not to convince Joe that she loved him. "But why not?"

"Well," Kitty said, "independence my not be the key to Joe's heart. You need to rely on him. Men like that. But you want to appeal to his other senses, too." The wives laughed and nodded. "What kind of underwear do you have?"

Ginger was shocked.

Vivian held up her hands. "Ladies, I have an idea. Let's have a wedding shower for Ginger, just among ourselves. Everyone can wrap up one sexy secret, a piece of lingerie that might make a difference. Kind of like a recipe shower only it will be for lovemaking. When shall we have it? Next Friday morning? Can everyone make it?''

Ginger stared at all of them, fear on her face. "But I don't think— You must not buy me anything. That's not necessary.''

"You can teach us how to make the cinnamon rolls in return. It'll be a Turner family secret. Will you do that?'' Amy asked.

"I'll be happy to, but presents aren't necessary.''

Several decided it would be good to ask their husbands and take them along on the shopping trip.

"Good idea,'' Vivian agreed.

Ginger gave up. Obviously she wasn't going to get any assistance from Vivian. Ginger knew only one thing for certain—they'd never celebrated a marriage in this way in Estonia.

After the family wives had gone home, Vivian took Ginger out driving. Her instructions were brief. She put Ginger behind the wheel of her own car in the middle of an empty parking lot. Ginger found it much easier than she'd thought it would be. Joe had always seemed so tense about the idea. Then after an hour of driving, Vivian took Ginger to the DMV beside the sheriff's office. After they picked up a booklet for her to study, they went back home, where Ginger read the booklet while Vivian fixed lunch.

Ed joined in the project when he came home for lunch. After going over some of the questions with her at the table, he took her out to drive also. She found him to be a nice, patient man, and once again remarked how much she would have loved to have a man like Ed as her father. Would Joe be the same kind of father?

She shoved such a thought aside. After all, she knew Joe didn't have family plans with her. His thoughts would be tied up with his new contract for quite a while.

Ginger enjoyed both lessons, but she couldn't see herself getting into the Honda he'd bought her earlier after getting her license and driving around without someone. Ed assured her she'd get used to it. Then he told her amusing tales about Joe's early driving days. Thinking of her husband as a young, awkward teenager was easier than thinking of him as her virile, sexy husband. But she couldn't get the latter image out of her mind. She went home several hours early to fix dinner for Joe.

First she took a shower, then dressed in one of her nice outfits, a light sweater that revealed her figure. Next she cooked a delicious meal of steak and potatoes, one of her husband's favorites. When he got home late, she assured him it didn't matter, though he kept apologizing, anyway.

"I'm sorry, Ginger, I'll try to be home early the rest of the week. It'll be no problem Friday. Dad insists all us guys play golf together once in a while, and he's suddenly chosen Friday for some odd reason. He called me this afternoon. I tried to put him off, but I couldn't."

"How nice," Ginger murmured, her cheeks red, feeling guilty, knowing she was ruining his workday for a silly reason.

"Mom said not to worry about you, she and her daughters would take care of you. She means all the wives. She always wanted daughters so she calls the girls that. You don't mind, do you?"

"No, Joe, I'm delighted."

She put his plate in front of him and sat down to eat her own food. "I hope dinner is all right."

"Dinner is wonderful, more than I expected."

He looked uncomfortable, and she changed the subject to stories of his outings with his brothers. Joe was quite a storyteller and she enjoyed herself. Still, she couldn't help but feel guilty for her easy day.

"I've been thinking, Joe. Maybe I should return to work at the country club."

He put down his fork and looked at her. "Ginger, do you need money? I didn't tell you I keep some in my desk drawer. I'll show you where after dinner. You could take whatever you need and enjoy yourself. Maybe take golf lessons at the club—but not with Clark," he hurriedly added.

"Why not Clark? Isn't he any good?"

"Uh, yeah, he's good, but he's got a reputation with—with single ladies."

"But I'm not single," she cheerfully pointed out.

"Just stay away from him, anyway," Joe growled.

Ginger thought he sounded jealous and she liked that. "I will, Joe." Changing the subject, she added,

"Did your father tell you he helped me learn to drive today?"

"When did he have time for that? He works all day, like me."

"No, he took the afternoon off and took me out for my second lesson. Your mother taught me earlier. He said I'm doing very well. Better than you when you were thirteen."

He glared at her. "You're much older, so of course you're doing better. But I intended to teach you."

The regret in his eyes meant a lot to Ginger. She reached out to touch his arm. "I would've preferred to be with you, but I know you had work to do. It was nice of them to help out."

He covered her hand with his, and the tingle from his touch ran up her arm. He lifted her hand and carried it to his lips. "Dinner is great."

"It's the least I can do." She raised her gaze from his mouth to his eyes. "Joe, I really think I should start my own business and bring in money also. Then I would feel better."

"If you do, people will think I can't support you. They'll think I'm a failure."

"Really, Joe, surely you exaggerate."

"Maybe, but that's how things work. Besides, I told you I have enough money."

"I know, but it seems wrong of me to take your money when you were only trying to help."

"You are helping. This meal is great."

"But I want to do more."

"You will. We're a team, sweetheart."

She smiled, liking the thought that they worked together for a dual purpose.

"So did you have a good day?" he asked.

She smiled again, thinking about the discussion with her sisters-in-law, and their opinions that Joe really did love her. "Yes, I had a wonderful day."

"Good. That's what I wanted."

"Then I guess we both earned our dessert." She cleared the table and brought an apple pie to the table.

"I'm a lucky man," he murmured, and leaned forward to kiss her lips.

She realized more than ever that she was a lucky woman.

Fifteen

Every day when Joe came home from work, no matter what time, Ginger had a great dinner ready for him. And a smile on her soft lips. And every day he asked her if the INS men had called.

And every day she said no.

"Maybe I should call them," he said. "We could choose the day they'll come out and finish our interview. It must be driving you crazy not to know."

"No, Joe, I don't think that's a good idea. I think it would irritate them and make them more suspicious."

He stared at her, wishing he could think of something to counteract those arguments, because he was going crazy. Every time he walked in the door and Ginger, more beautiful each day, greeted him with a smile and a terrific dinner, the more frustrated he became. But he'd made a promise....

He called himself all kinds of an idiot. Didn't he know women could drive a man crazy?

He'd thought of Ginger as too young for him. He'd thought he was just helping out a kid. But he didn't think of her as a kid now. Too often lately, he actually thought of her as his wife. But he'd promised not to touch her, just to help her get her green card.

But now things were different. Still, he'd keep his promise.

That was why he wanted to contact Mr. Fisher. Once she had her green card, when she didn't have to be married to him, then he could ask her to take back his promise. Then he could open the door and give her the opportunity to leave. The opportunity to live here, as she wanted, with him or without him. Then he wouldn't have to fight his urges every day and drive himself crazy.

Friday morning, they had a leisurely breakfast as usual. Mornings were becoming the best part of the day.

As they cleared the breakfast dishes, he asked, "What has Mom planned for you today?"

She gave him a startled look and hurried away. He followed after her. "Ginger?"

"Um, all the girls are going over."

"Why does that make you panic?" he asked, keeping his eyes on her.

"I—I'm teaching everyone to make my cinnamon buns."

"That's generous of you. Is that it? Is it a family secret you don't want to share? Do you want me to tell Mom?" He watched her carefully for her reply.

Relief gleamed in her eyes and he knew he hadn't found the right answer.

"No, I don't mind."

"Then why did you give me that look?"

"No reason. I hadn't told you about it and I

thought you would be unhappy with me. Do you like to play golf?''

He'd noticed her playing that trick before, changing the subject to something about him. He usually fell for it, too. She always acted as if she were very interested in whatever he liked.

''It's okay. Do you need to take some of my pots and pans to Mom's?''

''Oh, no, she has plenty of pots and pans.''

''I was hoping you'd go to the movies or something. Didn't you want to see that new chick flick?''

''Yes, but I thought you might like to see it, too. Amy said she and Bill usually take in a movie on Friday night without the kids. She wanted to know if you and I might go with them tonight.''

''I suppose we could, if you're not too tired.''

''You really don't mind?'' she asked, excitement in her voice.

He couldn't keep himself from swooping down for a kiss. ''Of course I don't mind. I'll tell Bill this morning.''

''Wonderful. When will you be home?''

''Probably around five. Take a nap if you want and I'll wake you up in time for the movie.'' He opened the door, moving away from her so he wouldn't be tempted to kiss her again.

''Wait! You're supposed to take me to your mom's,'' she called out.

He felt really dumb. Of course he was. How could he forget? But he knew how. His mind was on Ginger. ''Sure. You ready?''

"Yes," she assured him, and tucked her hand in the crook of his arm.

He hurried her out to the car.

Joe relaxed after he'd joined his dad and brothers. Then he told Bill he and Ginger were joining them at the movies tonight.

"You are?" Bill asked, sounding surprised.

"Yeah. Didn't you know Amy had asked us?"

"Yeah, sure," Bill said, but he sounded disappointed.

"I don't get it, Bill. Why ask us if you didn't want us to come?"

Bill muttered, "Amy asked you, not me. Friday night is our date night. Mom keeps the kids and Amy and I go out without them. I get her all to myself."

"So you want us to stay home?"

"No! She'd be mad at me."

As he pulled out a driver to tee up on the first hole, Rodney grinned at Bill. "Hey, what did Amy bring to the shower today, bro'? Kitty gave her a bottle of massage oil." He grinned at Joe. "You'll like it, Joe, and it can come in handy one night."

"Shower?" Joe asked, puzzled. "The wives are giving Ginger a shower? But massage oil isn't a standard gift for a wedding shower. More like towels or some steak knives."

Rodney laughed. "It's not that kind of shower."

"What other kind of shower is there?" He looked at his brothers and realized they were all laughing. "Okay, come on. Someone tell me what's going on."

"We thought maybe you needed some ideas to get things going. You know, you haven't ever been married before. After all, it's been a long time since you needed any encouragement."

"But Ginger is the one— Oh, no! You mean the girls are all giving her suggestions on how to…"

He paused as he considered what they'd said and his father finished off his statement "…to seduce you, son." Ed beamed at him.

"Damn it! They can't do that. Ginger's a virgin!" Joe turned around and headed for the parking lot.

Rodney called out to him. "Hey! Where you going? You just proved our point, bro'. You've been married to her for a couple of weeks and she's still a virgin?"

"Pay attention, stupid," snapped Joe. "I married her so she could get her green card. And I promised I wouldn't touch her. She's only nineteen!"

"And she doesn't want you to…you know?"

"No!" Joe roared, now really upset.

"But she told Amy she wanted you to do something!"

"Yeah, because she thought that would make her unattractive to that fifty-eight-year-old man. For no other reason."

His father grabbed his arm. "Here now, boy, no need to break up the party. Your mother isn't going to let her be embarrassed. If she thinks the girls are getting carried away, she'll call a halt. You know she will."

Joe stood there, his hands on his hips, trying to decide what to do.

"Shoot, you know Mom will," Rodney agreed. "Besides, Kitty doesn't know enough to embarrass anyone."

"Well, since you're expecting a baby in a couple of months, she must know enough," Ed pointed out.

Unbidden, the image of Ginger, pregnant with his child, came to Joe's mind. He knew she'd look beautiful. For sure he wouldn't protest, but Ginger might.

"Look, I'm sure they meant well, but Ginger's from Estonia. I shouldn't have left her with the wives."

"Get your wood out and tee off, boy. I'm not letting you mess up Vivian's fun. She already loves Ginger. She'll protect her better than you would in these circumstances."

After a moment, Joe, with a sigh, agreed. "Okay, Dad. I'm sorry, guys, if we've caused any trouble."

"Trouble?" Bill echoed. "Heck no. We've had as much fun as you will."

Ginger did take a nap when she got home at one o'clock, but it wasn't because the day was such a strain. She knew more than some of the younger wives, especially about birth control. Her mother said she didn't want her getting pregnant and adding another mouth to feed, as if her mother paid for the food.

The embarrassment came from her imagining doing what they suggested with Joe. She would have liked to do those things, if Joe would like it. Especially the candles. She loved the scented ones. And she already had several beautiful nightgowns from when she went shopping with Vivian. But she liked having more.

During her nap, she dreamed some delicious dreams. Her in a lovely blue silk negligee, scores of candles casting a romantic glow around the bedroom, and Joe leaning down to capture her lips in a toe-curling kiss. The kiss seemed so real...until she realized she was no longer dreaming. Joe had awakened her with a kiss and was sitting beside her on the bed.

"I'm sorry about the shower," he said softly. "They didn't mean any harm."

Harm? Ginger thought. It certainly didn't seem like harm in her dream.

"I appreciate you taking it that way. They don't understand about our agreement."

She got up and headed for the kitchen, figuring food would take her mind off the shower. "I think we only have about half an hour before we're supposed to meet Amy and Bill at your parents' house."

After they got to the theater, Joe discovered several other reasons to avoid the movies on Friday night. It was crowded. They found four seats together, but they had to squeeze in. Joe put his arm behind Ginger's seat so he'd have enough room. But halfway through the movie, Ginger was pressing against him because the movie depicted children in horrific circumstances. They were homeless and hungry, causing her to close her eyes and bury herself in his chest. At other times, she cried against him. When they got up to go home, he had both arms around her and she leaned against him all the way to the car.

"Did you like it?" Ginger asked.

"It was okay," he said, trying to hide his rapid pulse rate from holding Ginger all night.

"It reminded me of home," Ginger said softly. But everyone heard.

"You're kidding!" Bill exclaimed, staring at her.

"She probably doesn't mean about the children being harmed or going without food," Amy reassured her husband. "Right, Ginger?"

Ginger was surprised by Amy's words. "We didn't have a lot."

Joe pulled her even closer to his chest and shook his head at Bill over Ginger's red hair. "At least it had a happy ending."

"Yes, that's right," Amy agreed. Then she leaned over and kissed Ginger's cheek. "I'm glad you're staying here, Ginger, and not going back there."

"Yes."

In Bill's car Ginger started to sit up away from Joe, but he wasn't ready for that much distance. He pulled her back into his arms. He couldn't think about the violence without thinking of Ginger in such danger. He didn't regret what he'd done to keep her here, even if she decided to leave him. At least she'd be safe in the United States.

When the two of them returned to their condo, he

wasn't sure what to do, but Ginger pulled away from him and went to her bedroom, bidding him good-night. He would have at least given her a good-night kiss, but she didn't give him a chance.

Ginger leaned against the closed door. She couldn't do it. Amy had told her to lean against Joe during the movie. Cuddle, cry, pretend to be fright-ened. After they got home, she should use their closeness to lure him into her bed.

But the vivid scenes that reminded her of life in Estonia also reminded her how much Joe had done for her. How could she trap him into marriage when he'd already been so generous to her? Amy had no idea how much she'd already received from Joe. Nevertheless, the time in the movie had been delight-ful. But she had to stop it now, before they went too far. No more hugs, no more casual kisses. She didn't have the discipline she needed to be honorable.

After she got into bed, she tried to think of other things, but she drifted off wrapped in Joe's arms. And he held her all night long. In her dreams.

Ginger got up very early and immediately went to the kitchen and began making cinnamon buns for Joe. While she was waiting for the rolls to rise one last time, she noticed their neighbor collecting the mail from the mailboxes in the center of the condos. She decided to get their mail, too. She grabbed the key they kept in the kitchen window and slipped out of the condo.

It was a wonderful late-spring day, much warmer than April days in New York City, and most especially in Estonia. She had been blessed by coming to Mission Creek, Texas, and not just because Joe was here. When she didn't have Joe, she would still have the beautiful weather. But she didn't want to think about not being with Joe. She reached the mailboxes and unlocked their mailbox.

She took out the pile of envelopes. Joe seemed to have a lot of mail. She slowly strolled back, thumbing through the envelopes. She came to an abrupt stop when she found an envelope from the Immigration and Naturalization Service addressed to Virvela Turner.

Looking around, she walked over to the children's playground and sat in a swing before opening the envelope. A long legal-looking letter was folded around a small book. A small green book. Her fingers shaking, she looked at her picture, her name in black print, and the wording that gave her the right to stay in the U.S. and to work for her living.

Her green card.

Even though Mr. Fisher had told her it would come when he called on Wednesday, she hadn't really believed him. She looked up again, to be sure no one was watching her. She lifted her shirt and shoved the green book down the front of her jeans. Then she folded the letter and the envelope into her jeans pocket. After making sure nothing could be seen by Joe, she hurried back to the apartment. She felt like a teakettle ready to explode with steam. She could stay! They could no longer make her leave.

She could stay...

But not with Joe. She had to tell him that she didn't need him to get to stay. She needed him, and always would. But not for that reason. She chewed on her bottom lip. He wouldn't want her. He thought she was a child. He didn't love her. But she loved him. So much.

The door to the condo opened and Joe stood there. "Hey there!" he called, a smile on his face. "I couldn't find you."

"I went to collect the mail."

"I see. Anything interesting?"

Did he know? Had he seen her hide it? Of course not. He knew nothing. She rushed past him, but he caught her arm and lowered his lips to hers. She'd promised herself she'd avoid such kisses, but she opened her mouth to him. She couldn't pass up the opportunity to taste him again.

When his arms went around her, she came to her senses and shook her head. "We're outside, Joe." She pushed past him, into the condo, and put the mail on the table. "I must put the dough in the oven."

"You're making cinnamon buns?" he asked, his smile growing.

"Yes, it's Saturday."

Once she had the buns in the oven, she offered to call his parents to come have breakfast with them. She felt safer with company.

By the time Ed and Vivian arrived, the buns had

turned a fragrant brown and she'd cooked strips of bacon and round sausage patties. She had put on a pot of her special coffee, too.

The four of them lingered over breakfast for almost an hour. The family feeling she'd always longed for was there in abundance, she realized— until she told Joe her happy news. Then it would go away.

"Something wrong, honey?" Joe asked, staring at her. "You look sad."

"No, not at all. I'm very happy," she said briskly. "Mom, have you and Ed seen the movie showing at the theater?"

"No, we haven't, but my friend said it was a real tearjerker. Did you enjoy it?"

"Oh, yes, it was wonderful."

Ed growled, "How come you call her Mom and me Ed?"

Ginger stared at her father-in-law, worried she'd upset him. "I didn't know if you wanted me to."

"Of course I do, unless it— Your own father—"

"I never knew him, and I'd love to think of you as my father."

"Good, then call me Dad," he said, beaming at her. "Now, did you cry at this movie?" he asked.

"Yes, I did," she admitted.

"She said it reminded her of Estonia," Joe said softly. "Especially the fighting."

Ed patted her hand. "Oh, no, that's terrible. I didn't know things were so horrible for you there.

I'm so glad you're not going back. You'll be safe here.''

"She might not think so after several kidnapping attempts,'' Joe reminded.

"But she has you to keep her safe,'' Ed said. "In fact, all of us will fight for you if they try that again. Your entire family.''

Ginger felt so loved and protected, even without Joe joining in with his father's words.

"Thank you, Dad,'' she said. "That makes me feel so good.''

Vivian stretched out her hand to Ginger's and then Ed extended his to Joe and pushed for Joe to take Ginger's hand, so they formed a circle. A circle of love.

A knock on the door drew everyone's attention. Joe stood. "I'll get it. Probably some kid selling something for the school band.''

Ginger relaxed again, trying to tell Ed and Vivian how much she appreciated their warm welcome.

"Well, of course. You're Joe's wife,'' Vivian explained. "That makes you family.''

"Joe's a wonderful man. He's so patient and kind to me,'' Ginger said, her lips curling in a smile. Then she stood. "Dad, do you want some more coffee? Mom?''

"Oh, yes.'' Vivian stood and reached for Ed's cup. Then she followed Ginger into the kitchen. "Well, did Amy's plan work last night? Did Joe put his arm around you at the movie?''

"Uh, yes, Mom, but it didn't mean anything.''

"Oh," Vivian said in disappointment. "I thought for sure he would—"

"Ginger." Joe's voice stirred the quiet of the kitchen.

Ginger became alert. She knew Joe was angry with her from the tone of his voice. She couldn't imagine what was wrong, but she left Vivian standing in the kitchen and hurried to the breakfast room.

Only to come face-to-face with Carl Fisher, the INS man, and a very angry Joe.

Sixteen

Ginger stared first at Fisher, then at Joe, whose expression was fierce. Then Ed shuffled his feet and she realized they had an audience. That was the last thing she needed.

Clearing her throat, she said, "Dad and Mom, we'll call you later. We have a few things to work out." She kept a smile on her lips, but Joe didn't bother.

However, her in-laws took the hint and excused themselves. She took a deep breath and turned to the INS agent. "Mr. Fisher, I know you asked me to let you know the green card arrived, but I didn't realize it had until this morning. I forgot to pick up the mail yesterday."

"I'm sorry, but these are highly sought-after. I wanted to make sure it didn't get stolen. You do have it?"

Ginger turned her back on the two men, lifted her shirt and pulled out her green card, then turned back around. "Here it is."

Fisher reached out for the papers and Ginger surrendered them reluctantly to him.

"And I, of course, knew nothing about this," Joe

muttered, his voice harsh. "Why is that, Mr. Fisher?"

"I assumed your wife would tell you."

Both men again stared at her. "I can explain, Joe, but I'd rather do that when we're alone."

Joe's face was expressionless, but he nodded. She could figure out that he was through with her, but at least he wouldn't tell her in front of Fisher.

The official returned her green card to her and she gave a sigh of relief. "Thank you, Mr. Fisher, for all you've done for me. I promise I'll be a good citizen."

"I'm glad I could help. You two have been the most likely couple to actually make your marriage work." He smiled, but Joe didn't respond. "Ah, well, I guess you had your reasons for not telling your husband, Mrs. Turner. I've finished my involvement, but if I can help you in the future, just let me know."

He paused and watched them, as if hoping they'd confess their difficulties to him, but Ginger had no intention of doing so. It was going to be hard enough to explain to Joe without making him even madder.

Fisher told them both goodbye and left.

Before she could turn to face Joe, he went to his bedroom and slammed the door shut behind him.

This explanation was getting off to a rocky start, but she wasn't going to give up just like that. She went to the door and without knocking opened it. Joe was staring out the window, his back to her.

"Joe?"

He didn't turn around as he spoke. "Do you need help packing? Or do you want money? Just tell me how much. Let's take care of this as quickly as we can."

"I have money, Joe. My savings. I thought you would want to know why."

"No. I know why. I did this knowing I was too old for you. I thought you'd be honest, but I guess that was too much to ask. At least this way I get to say goodbye."

"I don't want to say goodbye."

"So that's too much to ask? Then go. Just go."

After several minutes of silence, he turned and stared at her. "Why are you still staring at me? I said you could go."

"I don't want to go."

He opened his mouth to blast her, but then he closed it and frowned at her. "Which is it?" he asked. "You don't want to go or you don't want to say goodbye?"

"Both," she said softly. "That is why I didn't tell you anything about the card. You promised me a year. I thought if I stayed with you for a year, perhaps we would become…fond of each other."

Ginger held her breath for his response.

"That's impossible!"

She gasped as pain shot through her. Her dreams crashed to an end. Joe didn't think he could love her, even with time. She ducked her head. "I see. Thank you for all you've done for me." She turned to leave.

"I have to go tell Dad and Mom—I mean Ed and Vivian—goodbye. Then I will be gone."

She hurried to her bedroom before he could see the tears sliding down her cheeks. There, she pulled out her old cloth bag and packed only the clothes she'd owned when she was a waitress at the Lone Star Country Club. She couldn't take the things Joe had bought. It would be impossible to forget him, then. When she turned to leave, she found Joe standing in the doorway.

"You're forgetting a few things, aren't you? Do you think I'm going to wear these?" he pointed to the outfits and nightgowns hanging in the closet.

"No, but Vivian will know someone who can use them. She won't let them go to waste." She tried to push past him, but he blocked her way and refused to move.

"Where are you going and how will you get there?"

"I plan on asking your father to take me to the airport. Please let me through."

"You're taking a plane?"

She kept her head down, hoping he wouldn't notice. "I don't know."

"I thought you wanted to live in Mission Creek."

"I can't."

His strong hand curved around her chin and forced her face to the light. "Why are you crying, Ginger?"

Almost shouting, she said, "I told you I didn't want to go."

"No one is forcing you to go."

Stupid man! She couldn't live in the same town with him when he didn't love her. "I have to."

"I can help you find a place to live and start your business."

"No! I have to leave."

"Ginger, you're too inexperienced to go out on your own. If I return to Chicago, will you stay here in Mission Creek?"

"Your parents would hate me. They're so happy that you've come home."

"But you know Mom and Dad love you," Joe insisted.

The tears returned. "I never had parents who loved me." She wiped her eyes with her hands. "I shouldn't have said that."

"I've got an idea. Why don't you stay here with me until the year I promised you is up? We'll get your business started. Maybe you'll even meet someone you want to marry."

"No."

"Why not? That's what you said you were planning to do."

Ginger drew a deep breath and took a big risk. "It's too late for that plan."

"What do you mean?"

"I've already found the man I want to marry." She couldn't look at him because she was afraid he'd read the expression in her eyes.

"Who?"

"You."

Joe stared at her, and she feared he'd stopped

breathing. "I know you think I'm too young for you, but I feel a lot older than Kitty and she's a year older than me. Life in Estonia is more difficult. It makes us grow up faster."

"You're right, you do seem much older than Kitty. And she's going to be a mother soon.".

"Yes, it's a good thing she has your mother and the girls to help her take care of the baby."

"She and Rodney have been married a year, so I guess she got married at nineteen, too."

"Yes."

He stared at her for several minutes, his face unreadable. Then he said, "Tell me again who you want to marry."

"You, Joe. I want to be married to you."

"Because it's easier, since we're already married?"

"No."

"Because I've got money?"

"No."

"Because I've got a great family?"

She smiled at him. "It's true, you do, but that's not why."

"Then why, Ginger? Tell me why."

"Because I love you. Because I want to sleep in your bed for the rest of my life." She opened her eyes wide and waited for his response.

"That's convenient, because I feel the same way."

Astonished, Ginger stared at him. "But you turned me down. I asked you twice!"

His arms went around her and he pulled her

against him. "I didn't think you wanted me. I thought you just wanted Leo to go away."

"True," she said in a considering manner. At Joe's frown she explained, "That was a side benefit, but not the most important one."

"So, what was the most important?"

"I wanted you."

Joe smiled at her. It seemed the most beautiful sight. "Then we've wasted a hell of a lot of time, young lady. Come on."

"Where are we going?" Ginger asked, holding her breath.

"To bed."

She didn't argue.

"Did I hurt you?" he asked softly as he rubbed her back. She stretched sensuously against him.

"Mmm, no. You gave me a lot of pleasure. And I'm willing to repeat it anytime you feel like it."

"Oh, really? That sounds like a challenge," Joe murmured, pressing himself against her. "I'm ready."

"I'm impressed. I thought it took 'older' men time to recover. Either I was misinformed, or you lied about your age," she teased him.

"I think my age is accurate, so you must be misinformed. Or there is another reason," he whispered in her ear. She pressed several kisses against the skin on his neck.

"What would that be?"

"It could be that you inspired me."

"Mmm, I like that idea. But I do have a concern."

"What's that?" he asked before he kissed her soft lips.

"How will Mission Creek ever get the design for their new project? You won't have time if I keep tempting you."

"I've got a plan." He began making love to her again and it took a while before Ginger could catch her breath.

"You'd better tell me what it is."

"Yeah, and I'm going to apologize for my plan before I tell you. I should've discussed it with you first."

"What is it?"

"We didn't use any birth control. I figure you won't be as eager if you're pregnant. I hope that doesn't upset you. I'm so old I can't afford to wait too many years for a family."

She ran her hand up his bare chest. "I think you're in pretty good shape, but I'm ready for a baby at once. Mom and Dad will be happy about that, too."

"Yeah. Mission Creek seems to be a swell place to make love. There seem to be lots of babies and lots of weddings here lately. We want to stay in fashion, don't we?"

"Yes, we definitely want to stay in fashion."

"That reminds me. I bought you a diamond ring back when we first got married. I think it's about time you wear it." He slid out of bed and went over to the dresser and opened a black box. When he got back in bed, he slid the diamond onto her finger and kissed her.

"It's beautiful, Joe, but I don't need it."

"I do. It's big so all the men in town will know you're taken. Forever and ever."

She kissed him. "Oh, Joe, I love you so."

The ringing phone interrupted their kiss. Joe stretched out an arm to reach it, and Ginger snuggled up to her husband.

"Yeah, Mom, everything's fine. Sure we can, in about an hour or two. Yeah, that will be fine." He hung up the phone and looked at Ginger. "I hope you don't mind. We're going to Mom and Dad's for dinner tonight."

Ginger looked at her watch. "We still have plenty of time."

He kissed her. "I don't think so. After we make love again, I have to show you a time-honored tradition in the Turner family."

"What's that?" she asked, raising one eyebrow.

"We're big on saving water. Conservation is very important."

"How do we do that?"

"Shower together," he informed her, his face serious.

"I'm glad to hear that. Conservation is very important," she assured him. "Do we time our showers?"

"Oh, no, darlin'. In fact, we shower twice as long so we'll be real clean."

"I can't wait."

* * *

Ginger squeezed Joe's hand. "Will we need to tell them that we're really married now?"

Joe chuckled. "No, if nothing else, when I fall asleep during dinner, they'll know."

"Joe! Surely you won't do that."

"No? Okay, the fact that I can't keep my hands off you and we go home as soon as we've eaten will be a clue."

"Joe Turner, don't you dare embarrass me," Ginger protested.

"We'll see. Could be you're the one who gives it away."

"Not me."

They entered the house, already filled with family. Immediately, everyone stared at them. "Our shower worked!" Amy shouted.

Ginger's face flooded with red.

Joe turned to his wife. "I didn't say a word, I promise."

"You didn't need to," Vivian said.

"Then how did you know?" Ginger asked.

"When I called Joe, he sounded more relaxed than he's been since you got married."

Ginger blushed again. "See, Joe, it *was* you."

Joe smiled sheepishly. "Well, I don't mind being the guilty one, as long as you're going home with me tonight, sweetheart."

"Every night," she whispered.

Several hours later, when Joe was ready to abandon his rowdy family to take Ginger home, he crossed the room to whisper his intentions in her ear. But he didn't get the response he'd hoped for.

"No, Joe, we can't!"

Stunned, he stared at her. "Why not? We've stayed long enough."

"I know, but Mom and I are concerned about Kitty. She's having some pains. I'm not so sure it's false labor."

"How would you know? You're only nineteen."

"I told you I've had lots of life experiences. I've delivered several children in Estonia."

Joe stared at his young wife in surprise.

"We didn't have many doctors in Estonia."

On cue, Kitty grabbed her stomach and bent over, a look of surprise on her face.

Ginger left his side at once, wrapping an arm around Kitty. "Come on, Kitty, I think you've gone into labor."

"No, that can't be. The doctor said I had more time, Ginger. It has to be false labor, but I didn't think it would hurt so much." Then she bent over again.

Ginger looked at Joe. "Go get your mother. Rodney, do you have your doctor's number?"

Rodney had been involved in an argument about baseball. "Do you want to go see him? Boy, you two don't waste any time," he said with a grin. "Kitty will call you tomorrow and give it to you."

Ginger sighed in exasperation. "Rodney, Kitty is going to have the baby tonight, hopefully in the hospital if you call her doctor right now. Her pains are coming about two minutes apart.''

''But, Ginger, you don't have any experience with babies,'' Rodney pointed out. About then, Kitty let out a cry.

Rodney yelped in surprise and ran to his wife's side. ''Are you all right, dear?''

''No! It hurts. Call the doctor!'' she gasped.

Rodney shook his head. ''But the doctor warned about false labor. We shouldn't disturb him before the baby really starts coming.''

''Rodney, the baby *is* coming,'' Ginger declared. ''Trust me.''

Rodney stared at her. ''But you're so young.''

''Call him, Rodney!'' Kitty screamed.

Amy escorted Rodney to the phone. ''Just tell the doctor and let him decide. He knows what to do.''

Bill told Joe to get his car ready. ''You've got the biggest back seat.'' Joe turned a little pale, but Bill told him Ginger would have to go with Kitty. ''She hasn't turned Ginger's hands loose since the first contraction.''

Joe nodded and went outside. Besides, they'd been the last to arrive. In a couple of minutes, Ginger and Kitty came out of the house and he hurried over to help them get to his car. As he turned back to his car, he saw Rodney, white-faced, come out of the house. ''Is Rodney going with us?'' he asked Ginger.

''No. Mom and Dad are taking him. He keeps passing out.''

Joe swallowed and hoped he did better when his turn came.

He drove quickly to the hospital, grateful he didn't run into any cops. Ginger stayed in the back, coaching Kitty on her breathing and making her feel much better, he could tell. His respect for Ginger grew.

They stayed at the hospital all night. About four in the morning, Rodney and Kitty became the parents of a sweet little girl, weighing four pounds and thirteen ounces.

"I hope she's big enough to make it," Ginger said in a shaky voice when Vivian gave her and Joe the details.

"The doctors say her chances are excellent," Vivian explained. "They're giving her oxygen but she'll be fine." Vivian looked at Ginger. "And thanks to you, so will Kitty. I'm not sure about your brother, though, Joe. He didn't last long in delivery."

Joe came to his brother's defense. "He tried, Mom, he really did. Kitty will forgive him, I'm sure. She didn't know he passes out at the sight of blood."

Ginger looked at her husband, his arms around her. "Do you?"

"No, I promise I don't."

"Good. I want you to see our child come into the world."

"You're pregnant?" Vivian asked, shocked.

"Not yet, but we're ready. I don't have any qualms about Ginger being too young after seeing her in action tonight."

Vivian smiled brightly. "You're right, son. You picked a good one."

He offered Ginger a quick kiss. "I certainly did, for a lot of reasons."

Coming through the neonatal unit, Rodney staggered over to Ginger. "Thank you for being there for Kitty tonight, Ginger," he said. "I wasn't much help."

Ginger hugged him. "You tried, Rodney, and that's what counts."

"I hope Kitty thinks that way."

"I'm sure she will."

"Well, I'm glad you're part of our family." He kissed Ginger on the cheek, then went back to his wife and baby.

"I'm glad you're part of this family, too," Joe murmured, pulling Ginger against his chest.

"I feel lucky to be part of this family. They're wonderful."

Vivian rallied everyone. "Come on. Amy made cinnamon buns like Ginger taught us, and she's got a big pot of coffee on. Let's go home."

Joe hung back. "Mom, I think Ginger and I will head for home. We'll call you guys later."

"Of course, dear. I'll give you an update on our newest Turner."

Once they got back in bed, Ginger fell asleep at once, her head on Joe's chest, her arm wrapped around him. He stayed awake a few minutes, thinking about the events of last night and how his wife had managed. She wasn't too young, as he'd worried.

She was absolutely perfect. As his eyelids shut, he reminded himself to tell her that tomorrow.

Joe smiled to himself. He may have been the last Turner bachelor, but he was one lucky man now. He'd waited for the best woman of all to marry.

* * * * *

*Don't miss the next story from
Silhouette's*
LONE STAR COUNTRY CLUB:
*LONE WOLF
by Sheri WhiteFeather*

Available March 2003

*Turn the page for an excerpt from this
exciting romance…!*

One

Hawk Wainwright walked onto his front porch, then stopped when he saw her.

The pretty woman next door.

She knelt on the grass, planting flowers in her yard. Curious, he watched her.

A soft breeze blew her hair across her face, shielding a delicate profile. She wore old jeans and a simple cotton blouse, but she managed to look ethereal. He suspected her eyes were blue, rivaling the color of the sky.

But the angelic beauty seemed determined to keep to herself. She never spoke to him, never met his gaze or acknowledged him in any way.

Not that Hawk expected special treatment. He wasn't the friendliest person in the neighborhood. Nor were folks drawn to him. Since his youth, Hawk had been considered an outcast. Then again, he didn't give a damn about socializing in Mission Creek. This town hadn't been particularly kind to him, even if it had been home for as long as he could remember. He lived on the outskirts of Mission Creek, and for good reason.

Hawk was the unwanted, illegitimate son of one of the richest men in the county. And being the

Wainwright bastard had taught him how to live on the fringes of society, how to thumb his nose at his daddy and his half siblings. They meant nothing to Hawk. Nothing at all.

Nothing but a childhood ache he'd long since outgrown. Standing six foot one with a set of broad shoulders and a pair of dark, unforgiving eyes, he was no longer a kid, hoping his prominent white daddy would notice him.

Thirty-three-year-old Hawk Wainwright was an Apache, a man who trained horses, rescued injured raptors and asked Ysun, the Creator of the Universe, the Apache Life Giver, to guide him.

And who was the pretty lady next door? he wondered as he started down the porch steps to retrieve his mail. And why was she so shy? So cautious?

Maybe she'd heard the gossip about him. Eight years ago, Hawk had dated a pampered, rich, breathtakingly beautiful white girl. But after they'd slept together, he'd discovered she had no intention of introducing him to her family or bringing him into her social circle. She had, however, treated him like a prize Indian stud, whispering quite naughtily that her roommate wanted a turn with him.

Stunned, Hawk hadn't responded to the lewd offer. But just days later he'd approached both girls at a local bar. After kissing one and then the other, he'd quietly told both of them to go to hell. Naturally, those hot, public kisses had culminated in a much-talked-about scandal.

But he'd learned his lesson, and these days Hawk

no longer felt the need to explore his Caucasian side by dating white women. Instead, he avoided them.

He glanced at his neighbor. She was as fair-skinned as they came, but she still fascinated him. He couldn't help but admire the way her gold-streaked hair caught the light or the way a spray of geraniums bloomed like a rainbow at her feet.

Let it go, he told himself. Stay away from her.

He turned and opened his mailbox, then sifted through the envelopes until an unfamiliar name printed on one of them caught his eye.

Jennifer Taylor.

He checked the address and saw that it was incorrect. The letter, bearing the logo of a fashion magazine, belonged to the lady next door.

Shooting his gaze in her direction again, Hawk weighed his options. Should he put the letter in her mailbox? Or use this as an excuse to satisfy his curiosity and talk to her?

Curiosity won, along with a self-admonishing curse. He was doing a hell of a job of avoiding her.

Stuffing his own mail in his back pocket, he headed toward her, cutting across the adjoining driveways that separated their houses.

"Jennifer?" he said, when he reached her.

She started at the sound of his voice, telling him she had been unaware of his presence.

Still kneeling on the ground, she looked up at him, shielding her eyes with a gloved hand.

"Are you Jennifer?" he asked.

"Jenny," she said, a little too softly. "I'm Jenny."

"I think this belongs to you."

She removed her gloves and stood. But when she reached out to take the envelope, she teetered.

"Are you all right?" he asked. She couldn't seem to catch her breath, and the sun flushed her skin, making it look hot and pink.

"Yes," she said, but her flushed face went pale.

Too pale, he thought.

The envelope fell from her hand, fluttering to the ground. And in the next instant, she was going down, too.